Saving Rome

Saving Rome

Stories by Megan K. Williams

Second
Story
Press

Library and Archives Canada Cataloguing in Publication

Williams, Megan K., 1965-
Saving Rome : short stories / by Megan K. Williams.

ISBN 1-897187-03-3

I. Title.

PS8645.I453S29 2005   C813'.6   C2005-904590-6

Edited by Charis Wahl
Cover design © Claudia Neri, Teikna Design Inc.
Cover photo © Evan Dion
Text design by Melissa Kaita

Printed and bound in Canada

*Second Story Press gratefully acknowledges the support of the Ontario
Arts Council and the Canada Council for the Arts for our publishing
program. We acknowledge the financial support of the Government of
Canada through the Book Publishing Industry Development Program.*

Published by
SECOND STORY PRESS
20 Maud Street, Suite 401
Toronto, Ontario, Canada
M5V 2M5

www.secondstorypress.ca

Contents

For Lorenzo

Home

S HE WASN'T THINKING CLEARLY.
The carbon monoxide from the traffic she'd been stuck in for the last hour was likely contributing to this high-frequency mental interference, this distortion that flared in her head like speaker feedback and made approaching reality with poise—her bottom-line goal these days—just a bit challenging.

The light switched to green. This changed entirely nothing: her car remained hitched to the perpetually stalled train of late-afternoon traffic on the outskirts of Rome.

Rome. The Eternal Hurdle. The hurdle that dares not be named. The hurdle she'd dared name a little too frequently. Often alongside words such as backwards, corrupt, chaotic, noisy, shit-ridden and the–land–that–time–forgot. Strict orders from Luigi: quit comparing. Every place is different. Not better, not worse. Just different. (Shut up and adjust.)

And who couldn't adjust? What was there to adjust to? Their stream of beauty-starved North American guests, confident and wholesome in their Gore-tex and wide-soled shoes, cried their envious approval. The food was so good! The buildings so old! The people so nice! So good-looking! So well-dressed! So thin! "If this is *la dolce vita*, I'll take it!" proclaimed a friend of her sister who had stayed for a week with her boyfriend and left a used condom under the pullout sofa as a token of the sweet time she'd had.

The traffic light switched back to red. She was going nowhere. She felt as if the signals from the thousands of unnecessary cellphone calls that were made each second in this city were being routed directly through her skull. (*Ciao* ... *Ciao* ... Where are you? ... I'm at the bank ... I'm on the bus ... I'm coming ... I'm almost there ... I'm here ... Put the pasta in to boil, *mamma* ...)

Marco, one of her five-year-old twin sons, began pummelling the back of her seat with a drum roll of kicks— further maltreating her abused body, strained from hauling around oversized children. His brother Luca giggled hysterically, egging him on.

"Stop kicking, Marco," she said. "Stop it, because I really want you to have the chocolate treat I promised, and if you keep kicking I won't be able to give it to you, will I?" It was a warbling, supplicant's plea. Marco responded as any self-respecting person would. He slowed the rhythm, intensified the impact. "Marco," she sang, "I'm warning you ... " When had she started warning in that melodious trill? When had she started tittering at the end of complaints?

She pushed the radio button, hoping for a song that would distract the boys. But it was the news, something about terrorism, police finding a quantity of something. Arsenal? Arsenic? Somewhere in the US? A bomb? She stabbed at the off button. Despite living in Italy for two years and working

2

part-time in a small museum, she hadn't been able to get a grip on this supposedly easy Latin language. The first year it had been funny. She couldn't even get straight *bene, allora* and *lui*—words that came up in every other sentence. "So who are Benny, Laura and Louis and why is everyone talking about them?" she had asked Luigi, seriously. It became their joke about just how clued-out she was. What Luigi didn't know was that she'd quit her weekly Italian classes after a month, when she was the only one in the class who still bungled the verbs "to have" and "to be." She kept going out on Tuesday nights—she'd booked the sitter anyway—but went instead to the English movie theatre, where her IQ felt higher.

A tinselly rendition of "Home on the Range" rang out.

"Mummy!" called Luca. "It's your phone! Get it quick!"

She plunged her hand into her purse on the floor of the passenger side and groped around.

"Quick!" the boys screamed, as if by answering her phone she'd avert disaster.

"I'm getting it, for Christ's sake!" she yelled, as she pushed the talk button.

"Whoa! Get you at a bad time?"

It was her sister from Toronto in her clear, crisp, middle-of-the-day voice. "Yes. No, actually. I'm stuck in traffic."

"Oh, drag."

"Yes, a major f-ing drag. The kids are bouncing off the roof in the back."

"So everything's OK then? I just sat down for lunch and read about the terrorist attempt."

"Oh yeah?" She had no idea what her sister was calling about.

"Terrifying to think they came that close to getting arsenic in the city's water system."

"Right. Where was this again?"

"*Rome.* Why do you think I'm calling you? Haven't you been following this?"

She hadn't. Following it would have required understanding the newscast. Or having the time to buy an English-language paper. Or having contact with an informed, English-speaking adult. Or conversing with her husband. Her sister, on the other hand, had no shortage of informed adults at her law firm. She had ample time to read the paper. And with a husband who participated in child-rearing and household tasks as if they were the very least he could do, she even had time to phone Rome to talk about what she'd read.

"No, I've been stuck in traffic."

"*All day?*"

The car in front of her swerved left onto a side street. She put her foot on the gas and surged forward into the space. The boys squealed.

"No, not all day. Just a good part of it. The bad part."

"Anyway, they think they were planning to poison the whole city, starting with the Americans of course. Can you imagine? Blows the mind what these guys come up with. Oh, hang on. Gotta take a call."

The line clicked, followed by a low-level buzz. She held the phone away from her ear and stared at her apartment building ahead. Just after the façade had been sandblasted, someone used it as a vast canvas for incoherent scribbles. Who were these people with cans of spray paint and arsenic and homemade bombs who had nothing to do but carry out these audacious acts? Who did they think they were?

Her sister's voice rose from the phone. "I'm back. Can't talk much longer. What were we saying?"

"The terrorists."

"Right. Anyway, say what you want, they're amazingly organized."

"And confident. I wonder where they get the confidence."

"Confidence?"

"Yeah. To express themselves like that. I mean, it takes self-confidence, don't you think? To inflict all that shit on everyone else."

"*Confidence*? Come on, Diane! These guys may be angry, but I'd hardly call them confident. They're losers. Even in their own network they're the bottom of the heap."

"Oh."

Her sister sighed. "So how are things going?"

A car idling at the curb ahead tried to pull out into the crawling traffic two cars up, but was blocked by another driver. A honking match ensued.

How were things going? Things weren't going. She was stuck. "Fine. Good."

Marco thumped her back, thumpity-thump-thump.

"And Luigi? How's he doing?"

"Fine. Working a lot." She covered the receiver. "I'm warning you … "

"Are you sure he's not screwing someone else?"

Diane guffawed, appalled but also in awe of her sister's ability to cut to a point. These brief and scattered phone calls brought familiarity, but lately, too, a mounting sense of danger.

Marco spiked her once more with his foot. With no premeditation she cut off the call, turned and whacked him. He shrieked. Then she hit Luca because he was within reach.

"It was Marco!" Luca screamed. "I didn't do nothing! You're mean!"

He joined his brother in tears.

"Anything," she corrected, with an eerie release of giggles. "Didn't do *anything*. Now simmer down while I find a parking spot, and you might just get those treats."

She was one block from home.

She'd started off all right that morning. Two cups of coffee and a plateful of shortbread cookies (breakfast in Italy!) and she was charged with enough ersatz elation to make it through the hour of hauling kids out of bed, stuffing their bodies in clothing, spooning cereal into their mouths and propelling their bums out the door. Then off to the nursery school, an affordable one run on the free labor of a fleet of aging nuns with enough self-perceived moral authority to tsk-tsk the mothers if their skirts were too short. But it was cheap and she was definitely no longer a wearer of short skirts.

Today the head nun had gently cornered her over the *grembiuli* for the twins. The nuns, like everyone else in this country, were too tactful to come right out and chastise her for not forcing the boys to wear the white lace-collared smocks that were the uniform of Italian preschoolers; but their unwavering smiles let her know she was failing.

"Where I come from, little boys don't wear dresses," she tried to explain. "They don't have clothes with embroidered bunnies on the collar. Girls don't even dress that way."

A miniature being, named Suor Giovanna, spoke to her with the special sympathy reserved for God's less mentally able creatures. "Here, instead, all children wear *grembiuli*. That way all the children are the same. There's no distinction."

Two pudgy, frocked boys, looking very sweet in their *putti* wear, were ripping the petals off a fake rose. Like so much here, it was form over substance

6

"Baah-baaah," she bleated, then added, "And *vive la différence*? What about that?"

She laughed. A covering-up laugh. She hadn't meant to bleat. And with a second's reflection she couldn't be sure that *vive la différence* wasn't a gay liberation slogan. But Suor Giovanna kept up her relentless smile and blinked just enough to convey that the mother in front of her had said something Not In Control.

"You yourself may like being different," the nun softly intoned, taking note of her hair, still wet and uncombed from her last-minute morning shower. "But is it best for your sons? We worry about them."

Luigi worried about her. Last night they'd watched a late-night talk show—women in gladiator outfits prancing around a couple of male politicians. They were having pan-heated frozen pasta dinners and a bottle of cheap yet good—this was Italy!—white wine. She'd become very adept at heating Italian frozen food products. They tasted every bit as yummy to her as the real thing, though she knew better than to admit that. Definitely not in the *a voce alta* category. At a barbecue with Luigi's colleagues from the newspaper she'd learned the limit of what she could say out loud concerning food. The group stood on someone's terrace in December smoking and rubbing their cold hands together and waxing romantic about their two thousand–year culinary tradition and the vast variety of bread baked in wood-burning ovens Italy still produced while other countries pumped out soulless white loaves. But this particular cook-fest wasn't taking off; it was freezing, the coals failed to catch and the mammoth slabs of Tuscan beef stayed stubbornly raw. She suggested the obvious: why not throw the meat in the microwave to speed things up? The group actually leapt away from her and yelped. Luigi fixed her with a forlorn gaze while the others' expressions slid into a kindly blend of curiosity and pity.

She tried to follow the talk show. The voices of the male politicians began to interrupt each other and overlap, building to an unintelligible eruption of feigned outrage. She watched the women seat themselves around the politicians, the camera lingering on their breasts. "So tell me again why these shows pass for serious intellectual debate?" she asked Luigi.

"God, can't we just watch TV and not analyze everything all the time?" Luigi edged away from her.

"But I don't get it. I mean, why can't you have a talk show without the tits? Other countries do it."

"I suppose because people here like it. And I suppose that reflects some terrible national defect. But, really, I don't care enough to discuss it again."

"I just don't get it, that's all."

"Look," Luigi said, his eyes bulging in frustration. "It's stupid, all right? But they're just boobs. I don't even see them anymore. Can't I just follow the debate without having to defend things I don't even see?"

"But isn't that worse? That you don't see them? It's like, not only are they ridiculous, but they're also invisible. They totally don't count."

"Would you prefer that I did see them? And paid attention?"

"Maybe. I don't know."

"What do you want from me?" Luigi groaned. "To change the whole bloody country so you can 'get it'?"

"You could try," she joked. "You could start by making English the national language. I'd get that."

Luigi turned back to the TV. One politician was standing, shouting down at another, spittle flying, while the host stood to one side, arms folded across his chest, with a bemused, helpless look on his face. She found it impossible to follow, even without the distraction of the women. She swirled her last piece of ravioli around her plate then swallowed it.

"You sure you're not depressed, *tesoro*?" Luigi said at last.

Depressed? She licked the sauce directly off her plate, so delectable it was. Luigi tilted his head to convey concern and rubbed her shoulder too vigorously. Her whole back ached. "Do you need a visit back ho—. A trip back?" He'd stumbled. One last consonant and she would have had him. Back where she came from could no longer be called home. Where they met and lived for five years before Luigi got transferred back to Italy could no longer be called home. Home was here. Home was now.

"No," she replied, "I'm just a bit tired. Actually, I think I'm starting to, you know, adapt."

"Wonderful!" Luigi said, rubbing more shoulder. "I'm so pleased."

While she was positive she was not adapting, she was pretty sure she wasn't depressed. Or if she was it was a mutant depression. A cross-cultural depression that didn't fully cross over. Or crossed too far. Double crossed. Nothing flowed, nothing fit. Her own body didn't fit; it bumped through doors, towered above *caffè* crowds and lurched down sidewalks like some Nordic peasant on her way to market with two round piggies in tow. She was too heavy, too thin-haired and too tall, even without pointy-toed, high-heeled shoes. She was appalled by all the high heels. Aghast that anyone had the nerve to produce them or the stupidity to put them on. She looked at the elegant, gorgeous, *self-possessed* Roman women and all she saw were their tottery heels: a grotesque and crippling parody of the womanhood they so splendidly achieved from the ankles up. Keep the bras—God knows she needed hers. Burn the heels.

She seemed to be alone on this issue. And a few others. Yet while her general not-fitting-in might have curbed her tongue and modified her behaviour, it had the opposite effect. It fired her up. She bore no resemblance to the so-sad-but-pretty faces on the Internet antidepressant ads she found herself clicking on lately: chin on hand, gloomy gaze into the distance. First, she was chuckling and guffawing far too much. Second, these expressions of contentment came with a desire to slug someone, throw a rock through a window or set off her own bomb.

Parking loomed.

Parking was a form of stalking, a deceptively languorous cruise toward a vulnerable gap in the steel and rubber landscape. No matter if the opening was lined with pedestrian stripes or blocked six other cars or appeared on a sidewalk or was sliced by a median or acted as a school entrance—only a Canadian seminarian on a first visit to the Vatican would think twice about parking in it. Notions of fairness, thoughtfulness and legality didn't apply. Eye and lunge, darling! Parking was a killer's game.

Incredibly, empty parking spots flanked her building. She signalled and with space to spare found herself employing a technique from her happy past: the three-point turn as taught by Young Drivers of Canada. (Oh, how simple life was then! Red lights that stopped traffic, signs that informed, the whole meal on one plate.) "Come on kids, out you get!" She reached back, unstrapped the booster seats, slid out her door, walked around the car and opened the curbside door for the sulky boys. Almost home. The drone in her skull dimmed.

A *carabiniere* appeared, stick-figure thin in his black uniform. He bore a striking resemblance to Bert from *Sesame Street*. She wished she could comment on the likeness, but her kids were only familiar with the bargain-basement Japanese cartoons with zero educational value shown here. The *carabiniere* shook his head. "*Signora,*" he said, not smiling. Cops and shopkeepers were the only non-smiling Italians she'd come across. And bureaucrats. "You can't park here."

"What do you mean, I can't park here?" she retorted. "I always park here. This is my building."

"*Signora,*" he repeated. "Please move your car. This building is under police protection. There's been a threat against American embassy employees and we have to clear the parking for security reasons."

It had to be Jeff, a young bachelor belonging to that nation who lived a floor below her. Only last week he'd paid her and Luigi a courtesy call to wonder aloud in perfect Italian if "there might be some way to lower the volume" on the twins' early-morning ruckus. Come again? This bland person who'd taken full advantage of his private Italian tutoring and so enjoyed flaunting it wasn't a day over thirty. He could not possibly be important enough to justify roping off all the prime parking. And to add insult to the injury of those who needed a car to get around and parking within a few blocks of their dwellings, who had part-time, underpaid jobs and children to chauffeur and mental bloody health to keep intact, Jeff did not own a car. Jeff was picked up by a driver every morning.

She scoffed loudly. Officer Bert's mouth formed a perfectly straight line.

"Listen, can't I leave it here for a little while?" she asked, hoisting Luca on her hip to underline her maternal burden. "Just until I get the kids upstairs? I can show you my ID and I promise we won't throw any bombs."

"Not even a fire cracker," piped in Marco.

"Not even a fart," added Luca, and made a fart sound. The twins giggled. He repeated the trick.

"*Signora*, get in your car and move it. Now."

Soooo, Luca back off her hip, back into the car, kids buckled back up, back behind the steering wheel. The static back on high in her head. She squeezed into traffic and rolled forward about two metres to a red light.

Then right turn, stall, stop, right, stall, stop, right, stall, stop, stall, stall … The boys began to fight over the torso of a toy monster. She circled for another seventeen minutes, shaking her fist menacingly between the boys to try to keep them from clobbering each other, passing her building and the *carabiniere* three times. Finally, just around the corner she spied a car liberating a parking spot. It beckoned—fresh and full of promise—and it would be hers as soon as the lights changed. She tapped a little rhythm on her steering wheel. She encroached onto the pedestrian crossing. Then a black Mercedes swept like a bat out of hell across the intersection in a flagrant, up-your-ass U-turn and screeched toward her spot.

Screw Young Drivers of Canada. She ran the red, cut off the Mercedes and plunged into the spot. Her spot. Hers, hers, hers! She cackled.

She was adapting.

"Come along, youngsters," she commanded in her

British schoolmarm accent. Back in control! She helped the distressed young'uns out of the car, urging them to simply tune out the angry honking of that nasty black car. They marched around the corner and across the street to their building. As they approached the entrance, Luca pointed. "Look, Mummy. The police officer who made us get back in the car is smoking. It's bad to smoke, right?"

"Very bad. His lungs are probably dripping with disgusting black tar."

"Gross!" said the boys.

"That's right. Gross."

The *carabiniere* stood with arms crossed, cigarette between thumb and index finger, casually chatting with another officer. He coolly raised one bushy Bert eyebrow at her and blew out a stream of smoke.

She gave him the finger.

"Come on, fellas. Almost there!" Into the building they went, past the nodding *portiere* and toward the elevator.

Definitely didn't plan that one. The cop's mouth had actually rounded in surprise. A cartoon "O". Funny, yet a dumb, dumb move. All into the elevator! Up, up, up and away to the refuge of home.

"Home sweet home!" she chimed as they burst through the door into their front hall. Door shut: *hoooome* free.

She yanked off the boys' shoes and threw their jackets into the hideous inherited armoire. "*Rome, Rome on the range ...* " she warbled. The boys joined in. "*Where the deer and the antelope play ...* " She made her way to the kitchen and the imported peanut butter that solved the snack issue as no Italian after-school treat could. "*Where seldom is heard ...* " She felt as ebullient and precarious as a hot-air balloon. "*An E-English word ...* "

13

The doorbell buzzed.

She ignored it.

Then it buzzed longer.

"Mummy," Marco said, "someone's at the door."

"Shush. It's probably gypsies asking for money. We don't want them to know we're home."

She sat the boys down at the table in front of sandwiches and milk. Gypsy blaming? How very Italian of her.

The doorbell buzzed again.

"But Mummy," whined Luca, plugging his ears, "the noise is hurting my ears."

She reached up into the high cupboard and pulled out two chocolate eggs. With a finger over her lips, she tossed them to the boys.

The sound had become a solid screech.

"My head is busting!" wailed Luca. "Make them stop!"

Unfortunately they'd just had electrical work done on the apartment. Luigi had inherited the place from his great aunt, who had done nothing to it but furiously dust and wax for forty years. It was a high-ceilinged, marble-tiled, darkly furnished, frigid apartment that had nothing modern in it except the TV they'd bought. And now this new doorbell, with its grating peal that could be heard three floors down.

She ushered the boys into her and Luigi's room, the farthest from the buzzing, tiptoed back out to the hall and grabbed their Lego bucket. The ringing stopped, replaced by thumping. She ducked and scurried back into her bedroom. She dropped to the floor, instinctively lying low.

The buzzing resumed. Luca put his hands back over his ears and rolled around, trying to drown the noise with humming.

"Gypsies are idiots!" said Marco. "I'm never going to give them any money. I hate them."

"Well," she said, feeling guilty about her contribution to stereotyping, "maybe they think we can't hear."

"Yeah, right!" scoffed Marco. "They'd have to be really stupid to think that. They'd have to be death to think that."

"It's deaf. And, yes, maybe they're deaf," she said, brightly. "Maybe these gypsies are deaf."

Obviously the *portiere* had told the police officer where they lived, but he couldn't have seen them actually enter their apartment. They could have gone to a neighbor's, if she had known any, or even back down the stairs while he was taking the elevator up. Both scenarios had about a five percent probability.

The ringing took on a staccato oom-pa-pa. The officer was pressing out a waltz, a light-hearted attempt to draw them out—like putting out cheese for mice—or a reflection of how crazed with rage he had become. Either alternative was ghastly. She tried to think it through. What was the worst that could happen if she opened the door and faced the music, so to speak? A very, very upset police officer would chastise her in front of the kids, which could give them a cop complex. Which might not be a bad thing. No sons in the force—she could live with that. But she couldn't bear her kids seeing her verbally pounded. She felt battered enough. She felt like an old pot.

The phone rang.

"What's going on there?" It was her mother. "It sounds like you're drilling for oil!"

"It's the doorbell."

"Good God! With all those lovely church bells you'd think the Italians could come up with a gentler doorbell."

"I can't really talk." She couldn't do anything. She felt paralysis seeping through her body.

"So go answer the door and let whoever it is in and then we can talk. I just need you for two seconds."

"I can't. It's a cop."

"A cop? What on earth—"

"Don't ask. Please. Were you calling about something in particular?"

"Yes. Dates. Sally and I are trying to figure out when to come. She finishes up teaching at the beginning of this month, but I have a couple of patients I can't leave until the end of the month. So that leaves early next month. Ten days, we were thinking."

"Right."

"We'd like to go to a spa for a few days. We were thinking Tuscany. Sally's reading that book. You know, the one about that divorced woman who renovates a house."

"Right."

"Yeah, well, it's got her all worked up about Tuscany now, although frankly I don't get it. Renovating is a nightmare. Why the hell you'd want to read a book about it is beyond me."

Luca appeared in front of her, his pants and underwear bunched around his knees, one hand tugging on his penis. She pointed to the bathroom.

"Come with me," he whimpered. "I'm afraid to go on my own."

"Go!" she mouthed. "Go!"

He stuck out his lower lip but shuffled toward the bathroom.

"So you think you can find a nice spa that's not going to bankrupt us?"

"I can try." Luca stalled in front of the bathroom door.

"Go in," she hissed.

16

The buzzing recommenced.

"Shouldn't you get that?" said her mother.

"No."

Standing in the hallway Luca peed all over his underwear and pants.

Her mother said, "How's the museum job? Are they paying you better now?"

"No." She motioned for Luca to step out of his wet bottoms. Distraught, he struggled out of them and made his way back into the bedroom.

"Is this because you're a woman? Did you tell them what you used to earn? What women earn here? That should shame them."

"Salaries are lower here. For everyone. Luigi doesn't even make—"

"So you keep saying. Anyway, Sally and I would like to take you to the spa. Our treat." A spa. Why did the thought clench her spine instead of relax it?

"I've got to go."

The buzzing stopped. Then started.

"Does Luigi know there's a police officer at your door?"

"Mum. I gotta go. Goodbye."

She grabbed a pair of underwear and some pants and dressed Luca again. Then she phoned Luigi.

"What's up?" It was deadline time at the paper, the worst hour to call.

She whispered above the buzz. "There's a problem."

"What?"

"There's a *carabiniere* at the door."

"A *carabiniere*?"

"Yes, he's after me." She laughed.

"What?"

"I gave him the finger."

"What?"

"They've blocked off the parking because the American guy downstairs received some threat. The cop made me move the car."

There was silence at the other end of the line.

"Hello?"

"I'm thinking," he said curtly. "How obviously did you give him the finger?"

"Oh, obviously. Yup, I'd say extremely obviously."

"*Merda.* Why do you do these things?"

"Do you think I planned it? He had a rotten attitude. He didn't laugh at Luca's fart joke. I mean, come on. Lighten up."

"Diane, *carabinieri* are permitted any attitude they want."

"OK."

"They're absolutely permitted."

There was a time not long after moving to Italy (though she didn't want to think about that) when he would have been delighted by her giving a cop the finger. He would have crowed about it at work, made it a much relied-upon classic of his party repertoire. His unpredictable, zany wife. Never a dull moment! Now she could barely walk into the room without feeling the sudden oxygen depletion from the huge bracing breath he took.

"OK, so police are allowed their attitude. And I'm not. Bad me."

Luigi sighed. "Go answer the bloody door. He'll give you a lecture or a fine and that will be that. Get it over with."

"I can't."

"Diane, you more or less told him to shove it. That didn't make him happy. Just answer the door."

"I can't."

"There's no way around it."

"Luigi, I need help here. A little *assistenza*?" Why didn't her voice reflect this? Why did she sound like she was having the time of her life?

"Go open the door. That's my *assistenza*. Deal with it."

The doorbell went back to straight buzzing. Maybe it wasn't the cop at the door. Maybe she'd open it and find the *portiere* with a package he'd forgotten to give her or a plastic toy one of the boys had dropped. She'd burst out laughing and clasp his hands with relief. Maybe the cop saw her raise her finger, but then noticed someone coming up behind him and assumed she'd given the finger to this other person because, after all, it was almost inconceivable that a mother with her kids would give an officer the finger. Or maybe … maybe she hadn't, in fact, given him the finger at all.

She had, of course. And she'd done it with his fellow officer looking on, which meant an official ego was involved. He had to go after her. But he would also have to calm down eventually. It would seem unprofessional, out of control, to keep buzzing like this. Wouldn't it? Although even if he left he'd likely come back the next day. Or wait for her, cutting a straight, black, furious figure in the apartment foyer. A figure that vibrated with righteousness and retribution. She pictured herself approaching him like a prisoner walking to the gallows. His hand appearing out of nowhere and slapping her hard across the face. A snapping crack. A crackling snap. Her dramatic fall, conking her head on the cold travertine pavement. Perhaps suffering mild brain damage—she could play with that part later. An ambulance would rush to the scene, attendants with thick, hairy forearms would lift her onto a stretcher and take her away to a hospital run by nuns who would spoon-feed her *stracciatella* (one bouillon cube, one egg, noodles and grated Parmesan cheese—a recipe even she could handle) and completely understand that she didn't speak Italian—of course she didn't; she was a foreigner!—and delight in communicating with her in sign language.

She knew this would not happen. She was aware that as an *americana* and a mother her chances of being slapped by a *carabiniere* were minuscule. This was Italy: mothers were revered. And yet she still feared it, expected it. Almost wanted it. She wanted release. From the mounting reproach for the gaffes and misunderstandings and inappropriateness and irritability and obtuseness that she'd expressed *so very badly*. From the interference that hummed or roared in her head, that dimmed but never ceased, that peaked in this screeching harpy of a doorbell that filled her husband's dead aunt's apartment and jammed against her skull, a pitch-perfect confirmation of her wrongness.

She opened the door.

Silence descended.

Officer Bert stood there, pale and frozen.

In a voice that came from somewhere far down his throat he said, "I saw what you did."

"*Allora?*" A good word. A six-letter, ball's-in-your-court-now, all-occasion word. A word she could pull out and employ with confidence. No longer Laura, but *allora*: So what do you want? So what's next? So what? So? A word she could pronounce.

"*Allora? Allora, signora,*" he hissed. "In front of your children!"

She offered up a weak smile. "They've seen worse."

The officer regarded her grimly. She sighed and leaned against the door frame. She could hear the sound of a TV cartoon, the wafting echo of the *portiere* on the ground floor chattering with a workman about some repair. A surge of warm dusk air blew in from an open stairwell window. If there weren't a police officer staring her down, this could qualify as her first quiet moment of the day.

"I could charge you," he said.

"Yes."

But he did nothing except sigh and lean against the wall, arms crossed. Tired. She thought of his day, standing on a street corner, holding a machine gun and shooing away irate drivers.

Her back throbbed.

"Look," she began. "I don't know how this works. Do I pay a …?" What was the word for a fine? She couldn't recall. He'd think she was offering a bribe. She'd offer one if she only knew the word.

But he shook his head and made a "tsk" sound, Italian shorthand for "no." He reached into his jacket pocket, pulled out a packet of cigarettes, shook one out and lit it. He inhaled and blew out the smoke. "Tell me something," he said at last.

She nodded. Here it comes.

"I've come across a few women like you. Wives of diplomats and so forth. Nice apartments like yours," he said, jerking his chin toward the armoire visible in the front hall. "Tell me, why are you all so mad?"

"Mad?"

"*Si.* Angry. What did you expect when you came here? Everything roses and flowers? Everything just like home?"

She thought of all the things she could say, things that if located and given form would come spewing out, like some printer gone haywire. Reams and reams that would fill the stairwell and the foyer and roll out onto the car-covered Roman streets.

Yet she was unable to articulate one, even to herself, aware that her inability to express what she felt went beyond mere incompetence in this language, this culture. She'd lost the code to her thoughts and feelings and wasn't sure it was worth finding, so clunky and uncertain and inchoate they had become. She wanted to explain this to the *carabiniere*, who looked drained and defeated inside his starched uniform, as weary as she felt. But she couldn't. Not to him, not to Luigi, not to anyone.

So she said, "I think I expected more parking."

The officer stared at her—either a disappointed or a conceding stare, she couldn't tell. His head moved almost imperceptibly up and down.

"*Ho capito*," he said. "I understand."

He sighed one last time and descended the stairs.

The twins weren't watching TV. They stood in the hallway, their backs against the wall.

"Mummy," Luca said, "are they gone?"

"Yes, they're gone."

Luca's chin trembled. He came to her with his head down and wrapped himself around her leg, crying.

Marco frowned. "I heard who was at the door," he accused. "Those weren't gypsies. That was the police officer you did the middle finger at. I saw you do it."

"Gave the finger to. Not did. Gave."

He stared at her. "Gave."

"How come you know so much and you're only five?"

"I dunno," he said, before starting to cry himself and moving toward her reluctantly, her little tough guy.

She lowered herself to her knees and held a boy in each arm while they sobbed. As she rocked their warm, quivering bodies against hers, she wondered when she had last cried. She couldn't remember and realized that she also couldn't remember the last time she had really, truly laughed. And she wondered if crying and laughing were a form of indulgence. For those who had enough mental space and time and belief in themselves. And she wondered how she'd ended up in this spot, and how she might get out of it.

Then she realized she was hungry and that the boys must be hungry and she wondered if the corner store would still be open so she could pick up some frozen fish sticks and peas for dinner, or if they should go to the Chinese restaurant down the street where the food was nowhere near as good as it was in the Chinese restaurants where she came from. But it was cheap and good enough to give her the incentive to stand up and keep moving because she knew it was important, for now, that she not stop.

Pets

AFTER SEVERAL WEEKS of my daughter pestering me for a hamster, I took her to the local pet shop. We live in an upscale Roman neighbourhood on the edge of a majestic park surrounded by towering umbrella pines. It's gorgeous. Every time I take the garbage out to the bin on the street or buy bread at the nearby bakery I thank my lucky stars. But I am always amazed that upper-class Romans feel no civic shame in letting their dogs' waste broil in the sun for the rest of us to inhale and step around. Strolling here is like treading through a fetid minefield.

The pet shop sits on a little side street by the park, sandwiched between examples of Italy's two dominant versions of femininity: a high-end children's clothing store displaying miniature linen outfits, starched and springy; and a lingerie store, its window strewn with limp triangles of dark fabric. The pet shop is hard to cruise by with kids. They stop and ooh and ah and point out their favorite little animal. Tuesday is especially hard: there's usually a new shipment of rabbits or gerbils, sometimes the odd pathetic puppy huddled in a corner. By Friday only one or two little beige creatures remain, which I assume get mixed in with the next batch, and so on.

The day Ella and I went to the shop, the choice wasn't great: four sandy-colored hamsters, each with a blurred grey line running down its spine. We squeezed through the cramped entrance alcove stacked on both sides with cans of dog and cat food. Stepping into the shop felt like undergoing an atmospheric shift. The harsh daylight and motor noise from the street ceased and we were enshrouded in a dim, dank melange of wood chips, animal piss and rubber.

When my eyes adjusted I saw a skinny older woman hunched beetlelike in a lawn chair beside the cash. She wore faded jeans and chunky white runners sprouting tinsel laces. Cottony strands of hair hung down the sides of her face. In one shaky hand she held a cigarette with a squiggle of smoke lifting off it. In the other she clutched a cone-shaped ashtray fashioned out of a scrap of newspaper.

I inquired about the hamsters.

She rolled her eyes then pivoted them towards the back of the store, where a guy was hanging rubber toys on a display stand. He had the same long, fluffy hair, though his was thinning, and wore a T-shirt with *Hustler* across the chest in fluorescent pink cursive. The sleeves were ripped off at the shoulders, showcasing sausagey arms and a lizard tattoo. His jeans were high on the hips, skin-tight and worn almost white at the crotch. If it weren't for his eyes, which were grey and enormous and emanated a gentle, disarming candor, the net impression might have been lewd. Perhaps it was the context, but he brought to mind Milky, a huge white cat with a terribly macho swagger, who had belonged to our next-door neighbors when I was growing up. Despite their sexed-up presentations, both Milky and the pet-shop guy gave off an aura that hovered between sweet and stoned. Even his voice was high.

"*Si, signora,*" he said, shuffling slowly around the small counter. "The hamsters are at the front."

He pulled the cage from the window display and lowered it to the floor. Ella's little fingers twitched with excitement. She dipped and pulled her hand nervously in and out of the cage through the trap door on the top. The guy chuckled in a quiet, private way. He reached into the cage, picked up one of the hamsters and stroked it with his thick thumb. When the creature turned flaccid, he held it out on his palm for Ella to pet.

"Have you ever had a hamster before?" he asked her.

Ella, mesmerized, fingered the hamster's back and shook her head no. He opened his mouth and breathed in as if he were about to speak, then sighed and smiled enigmatically. He and Ella joined their outstretched hands at the fingertips and let the hamster scurry back and forth along their arms.

"So what all do we need?" I asked.

"That depends, *signora,*" he answered, keeping his attention on the hamster. He had yet to make eye contact with me. "How many hamsters would you like?"

"Two!" said Ella.

"One," I countered

Ella did her best sweet-little-girl plea. "Please, Mom. Can't we get two? They'd keep each other company."

"No way."

I had a good reason to say no. We'd been to a birthday party for one of Ella's school-friends the week before. Ella goes to a for-profit English-language school that makes a killing off international agencies paying through the nose for their employees' children to learn the globally dominant language with a heavy foreign accent. The mothers are like me, traipsing after their husbands as they climb whatever career ladder they're on. Most of our husbands' employers have a no-spouses hiring policy—in theory this prevents nepotism; in practice it cuts off qualified women from jobs. At parties we sit exuding frustration and boredom, cringing at the noise produced by screaming eight-year-olds. *All that education for this?* I try to stay away. But Ella had begged me to take her to this particular party. In a huddle of mothers I sipped cheap Prosecco and ate stale chips while the birthday girl's mother tried to sweet-talk us into taking home a bunny. The two rabbits that she had been assured were female were humping away in one cage; six newborn bunnies squirmed in another. There was no way this was going to happen to me.

"Just one," I repeated.

"OK. You'll want a single cage, a water holder, some litter to put on the bottom and a box of food," the pet-shop guy said. Then he paused and added, "You'll need to refill the water holder regularly. Sometimes people forget."

"Got it."

He collected all we needed and tallied it up on a yellowing pad of paper. We paid, and when we said goodbye, our arms loaded with rodent paraphernalia, he bade us farewell with a wistful smile. The mother, who hadn't budged, jerked her chin up and called out, "Goodbye, *signora*. Children love animals!"

We had moved to Rome from Toronto a year earlier when Ted, my husband, took a posting with a global food agency. Ted specialized in emergency relief, the organizational side of getting food to famine. Before taking the Rome contract he had been a commodities trader in wheat. His job change wasn't as radical as it appeared: he was still in wheat, just on the buying end and no longer primarily in it for the money. With the new job, people appeared more inclined to like him and at parties tended to display a nodding deference to his opinions on world affairs. In Rome I taught English privately, something I'd never done before and for which I showed no aptitude; but it was a reason to leave our apartment other than having to escort Ella to school or purchase appetizing comestibles. We'd taken on the former tenants' Ecuadorean cleaning lady, so there wasn't even much housework to do.

This was my big break; for the past ten years I'd worked long hours at an architecture firm that specialized in shopping malls and small industrial complexes. I needed a change. What better place than Rome? we said. The move was also a chance for one of us—me—to spend more time with Ella. I could perfect my Italian, too, which I'd taken at university as an easy elective, and pursue an earlier interest in Etruscan archaeology. But really? These were *ex post facto* benefits. The real purpose of the move was to help Ted inject meaning into his life through saving other lives.

The lives of animals didn't factor into the plan, and the irony of nurturing a rodent after years of killing them didn't escape me. I must have bagged dozens of half-dead mice in those atrociously effective sticky traps without an ounce of regret. But Ella seemed to love her little envoy from the animal kingdom intensely and I did my best to humor her. She didn't tell me much about how things were going at school, but she rarely brought kids home to play, and I suspected her wanting a pet had more to do with missing her old friends than the urge to commune with another species.

I tried to establish some ground rules: no taking the hamster out of the cage without asking, no holding it while walking. That was useless of course. She had the animal out of the cage constantly, stroking it, poking its tummy and sticking it up her sleeve and closing her eyes in hushed pleasure as she felt it scrabble its way up her arm and down her back.

At first I'd been determined to spend as little money as possible on the creature. Buying the smallest cage had initially seemed sensible, but I began to be concerned that the hamster was understimulated. It climbed endlessly up and around the cage bars seeking a way out, and worse, it gnawed on the bars at night. Each morning I could discern a new stretch of steel shining through the bars' yellow plastic coating. I thought a hamster ball might offer it relief from all the confinement. Ted was in town between missions. I phoned him at work and asked him to pick one up on his way home.

"Is this totally necessary?"

He was preparing to leave the next day for Afghanistan and was under a lot of pressure. Because of his job, Ted's world had been reduced to two categories: the totally necessary and the not-to-be-bothered-with. This could get irritating.

"No," I said. "Very little is."

He sighed and said he'd do his best. He came home later that night with a sphere the color of a cherry Lifesaver. This worried me. What would be the psychological effect on the hamster of being stuck in a ball of that intense a red? Ted said he thought most animals were color-blind and that, anyhow, it had been the last one in stock. Ella was thrilled with it. She shoved the hamster in, snapped the trap door shut and launched the ball across the living-room carpet. The hamster flopped around like a sock in a dryer. When the ball stopped rolling, the creature lay frozen on the bottom, tensing for the next round. We told Ella to lay off, and when the hamster realized another assault wasn't coming, it began to lean its weight against the inside of the sphere, rolling it cautiously forward. The three of us watched the ball waft jerkily across the floor. It was eerily mesmerizing, as if the ball and not the creature within it were alive.

That night Ted and I drifted off to sleep in the dark to the sound of the hamster in full charge, bumping and gliding down the hall outside our bedroom.

"What did you think of the pet-shop guy?" I asked.

"I think he looks like a serial killer."

We snorted; Ted had hit the nail on the head. That curious smile, the uncanny affinity for children, the elderly mother hunched in her apologetic curl. And all those helpless, trusting creatures. I hadn't been in Italy long, but long enough to comprehend that a young man with a gentle but ill-defined look in his eyes who ran a pet shop alongside his aging mother was firmly within social norms. Hardly something to chuckle over as you drifted off to sleep. Where we came from, alarm bells would ring.

I didn't think about him again until a few days later when our paths crossed as I made my way home from a tutorial session with a police marshal. The marshal and I had been through a labored discussion in English about the laws pertaining to dog shit. Using discreet euphemisms such as dogs' "little needs," he had reassured me that it was counter to the regulations for owners not to pick up after their dogs, with a steep penalty for those who got caught. I wanted to point out that penalizing offenders would necessitate officers doing more than stand around smoking, looking bored and handsome, but I wasn't sure he'd appreciate the observation.

So the "little needs" issue was on my mind as I walked along the narrow alley leading out of the park toward home and noticed a German shepherd defecating. I debated whether to ask the owner to pick it up. In my first months in Italy I would raise an eyebrow, even point. When this proved ineffective—Romans are great at acting oblivious when it's convenient—I would say, "*Signore, per favore* ... " My exasperated "please" was invariably interpreted as an assault on human liberty and self-expression. Each time, I was accosted with a torrent of verbal outrage accompanied by all those wonderfully articulate Italian gestures for which I was no match. I soon learned to say nothing.

Then I realized who this particular dog-owner was. I hadn't recognized him at first because he appeared so poised. Away from the stuffy shop, his gnomelike mother and the parade of pet responsibilities, he looked relaxed, confident even. A man content to be alone with his dog. Almost cool. He pulled out a plastic bag, bent over and scooped up the shit, and he did it with such grace and fluidity of movement that I couldn't help but be affected. Touched. This wasn't someone to chuckle about; this was someone to take seriously.

I smiled.

But he didn't smile back; he stared right through me. I kept walking, my grin feeling foolish, thinking, of course he didn't recognize me. Why would he? I was just one of the dozens of mothers who reluctantly entered his little pet world to satisfy the cravings of their children. Even with my accent and North American jogging shoes I was as interchangeable to him as the foreign nannies pushing strollers and the chic housewives were to me. Outside his store he hadn't given me a second thought.

On Saturday morning I went into the kitchen to find Ella sitting cross-legged on the floor cradling the hamster in the palm of her hand. There was a furtive look about her.

"I think she's tired after rolling all night," she said.

I bent down to have a closer look. The creature was breathing and looked alert, but was unusually still.

"Did you drop her?" I asked.

"No."

"Did you squeeze her too tight?"

"No, I didn't," Ella said in an injured plaint. She was lying.

I went to have a shower and when I re-emerged Ted was sitting on the bed beside Ella holding the hamster.

"Look!" he said, grinning. "He's so relaxed! He's lying on his back like a kitten."

"It's a she."

"She, he, whatever," he mumbled, circling her tummy with his index finger. "Hey, little critter … "

Then he frowned and looked up at Ella. "Are you sure it's all right?"

"I don't know."

It wasn't. It was dying and in fifteen minutes it was dead. Ella's face, which was already strained with worry, crumpled into despair. For the next two hours she revelled in pathos—wailing, screaming, beating her fists against the bed and pulling at her hair. (Where did she learn that?) Then I proposed we go trampolining in the park and she snapped out of it.

The following Tuesday I headed back to the pet shop alone.

The guy was behind the counter and his mother sat in her spot by the cash, staring blankly at dog leashes dangling from a display case. She turned her head and nodded knowingly, as if she'd been expecting me. Had we looked like a family whose pets didn't survive? I approached her son and told him about the hamster.

He tilted his chin to the side. "Do you mind if I ask you how she died?"

What struck me about his question was that the "do you mind" part wasn't a figure of speech. He really was asking if I minded being asked. I didn't mind. In fact, as I told him about Ella's suffocating affection for the creature, I realized that I'd come to do just this: to confess.

And as I'd somehow anticipated, he was an exceptional listener. He nodded slowly, appearing saddened by the hamster's end, but not condemning of us. He'd sell us another hamster, of course he would. But perhaps he could suggest a few things? Things like never squeezing the hamster, for instance? Or always sitting down securely when picking up the hamster? Never shaking the cage when carrying it? He spoke to me in the hushed tone he must have used for the spellbound school children who passed through his shop each week, and I drank in the condescension like a baby at the breast.

When he was through I held out my hand. "I'm Elizabeth," I said. He reached out his and we brushed palms.

"Massimo."

I decided to get two hamsters this time, after Massimo assured me in his understated way that they were both females. He also promised that he would take any babies if they did turn out to be male and female, which I thought was particularly decent of him. Because there were now two, I decided to exchange the small cage for a two-level affair with tube-shaped passageways, a few plastic palm trees and a mini treadmill. I couldn't take any more of that desperate gnawing on the bars.

Ella was doubly delighted with her new hamsters, although she still showed flashes of guilt over having killed the first one. She wrote little notes to the dead creature and asked if we could attach them to helium balloons to send them up to her in heaven. Replacing the first one so quickly with two new ones helped ease her bad feelings. But it was right that she was experiencing some guilt—she had, after all, squeezed the life out of it—and I didn't want her thinking of living things as disposable, nor as easily replaceable. Yet, hamsters were, weren't they? You could replace them in a second.

The new ones were younger than our first and spent most of the time lying together. I thought they would start to explore the cage once they got used to it, but after several weeks it became clear they were permanently shell-shocked or depressed. They hardly budged. Ella lost interest in them. I stuck the cage in the corner of our living room behind a plant. I couldn't bear to see the immobile little humps of fur.

But I felt their presence and this was disturbing. They began to feature in my dreams. One night, several weeks after we got them, I dreamt of an immense hamster that split in two. The fissure was gory, with blood and fur and a viscous kind of afterbirth spilling out. One of the hamsters emerged intact but the other was so sickly, so deformed, it could barely move. The healthy one dragged the sick one around the room with its teeth. It kept trying to squeeze under the door to our bedroom, but got stuck. I tried to pull it loose but a leg snapped off in my hand. I woke up at that part.

In another dream we'd gone away on holiday and forgotten all about them. We left them for months without food or water. Just as we were coming home, I remembered. I was sure we'd find a pair of brittle skeletons wrapped in a scrap of fur. Actually, I was hoping we would, hoping that the hamsters had died early and quickly, that they hadn't suffered. But when I peered into the cage, there was only one and it was still alive, though too weak to move. It transfixed me with the round, bewildered eyes of innocence betrayed. Then I realized it wasn't a hamster at all, but a little girl.

I decided to take the hamsters back. When Ella was at school one day I picked them up with a dish towel (I couldn't bear to touch them), put them into a shoebox and carried them back to the pet shop. Massimo was rearranging plastic dog bones. His mother sat beside the cash, pinching a smouldering cigarette. She nodded as I approached the counter.

"I'd like to bring these back," I said. "I don't know if they were separated from their mother too soon, but they're despondent. They hardly move."

Massimo took the lid off the box and fixed the hamsters with a forlorn gaze. It was hard to tell if he was feeling sympathy for the creatures or was irritated at having to take his little charges back. I assumed the former.

"Hamsters are nocturnal animals. Are you sure they're not active during the night?" he asked.

"I don't think so. I'm a very light sleeper and I've never heard a peep from the cage."

"What do you expect? They're hamsters!" the mother piped up. "They're not supposed to do much. Move around the cage a little. They're for children." She gawked at me like I was a slow learner then shrugged and turned back to face the front door.

Her son said nothing, though his frown deepened. He silently scooped up the creatures and disappeared into the back of the shop. When he came out again he held a plump, cream-colored hamster in the palm of his hand. He lowered it into the shoebox.

"Try this one. She's been in a cage by herself because she was biting the others. She might work out better."

"I don't think I want a biter," I said.

He jerked his head back slightly, closing his eyes— that Italian gesture that says, "Please, I'm right"—and stuck his hand into the shoebox. The hamster sniffed his finger and then climbed into his palm. "She just bites other hamsters to show them it's her territory, but on her own she's fine. And she's gentle with people. Look."

His mother looked over again, her eyes hopping back and forth between us. She lifted herself slowly off her chair and shuffled out of the store.

I tried to catch Massimo's gaze, but he was engrossed in watching the hamster loop around his hand. I stood silently, watching the animal as it moved, breathing in the musky pet-shop air. There was such an intimacy, such a delicacy to their interplay that a pang of longing shot through me. I yearned to have some gentle soul chuckle fondly over me, over my antics. For just a moment I was jealous. Jealous of a hamster.

"Are you getting any dogs in soon?" I asked.

He looked me directly in the eye for the first time. "We should have some beagle puppies in next month."

"Could you put one aside for us?"

I didn't mention the dog to Ella or Ted. I didn't want to deal with Ella's expectation or Ted's opposition. Ted hated dogs. While he'd never admit it, part of his aversion stemmed from snobbery. His father was an aristocratic Viennese who saw animals in the house as evidence of peasant roots. But Ted's younger sister once confided to me that when he was a boy he used to hide behind her any time a dog or cat came near. A small caged animal was about all he could handle. That and thousands of starving humans.

Hamster number four worked out much better. She was smart and learned within hours how to escape from the cage. Ella and I spent a frantic afternoon trying to locate her. It wasn't until we were eating dinner and saw her scamper across the kitchen that we discovered her hideout under the fridge. We placed a wedge of apple about six inches from the fridge to entice her out. It worked. Ella swooped down and plucked her up before she could spin her fat little body around on the slippery floor. We returned her to her cage and placed a heavy book against the side we thought she'd escaped from.

When we checked the cage the next morning, she was no longer there. Again, we combed the house. I had Sonia, our cleaning lady, poke a broom under the kitchen appliances while Ella sprawled on the floor looking under the couches and beds. I checked behind the bookshelves and under pillows. Ella suggested a Hansel and Gretel strategy, a trail of apple wedges from the fridge to her cage. The next morning we discovered several of the wedges missing and knew at least that she was alive. I then put out a little bowl of water and a small dish of cereal. Each morning we'd find the dish disturbed and a scattering of crumbs around the kitchen. We also began to find dust balls in odd places. I pointed them out to Sonia. Her eyes widened and she assured me she thoroughly mopped the apartment each time she came. I could tell she was perturbed by my implicit accusation, so I didn't push it. It took me a while to figure out that the hamster dragged them out with her from under beds and couches while roaming at night. Our free-range hamster.

Soon she started to appear in the late afternoon and when we didn't immediately pounce on her as she zigzagged across the kitchen floor, her scurry developed a certain casualness. She'd dash, then slow down. Ella or I would kneel on the floor with a little piece of bread or cracker, waiting for her to come. And she did, finally, in a kind of two-steps-forward, one-step-back rodent mambo. She even began to climb up into my palm and munch on her flakes there. I always set her back in the cage, but by this point it was merely to reassure her that she had a home with food and water. Each time, she escaped.

Her escapes were feats of exceptional agility, tenacity and intelligence. She usually made her breakout between the same two bars, though you'd never guess they were slightly wider apart than the others. She would poke her head through the bars and hook her paws onto the next vertical. Then she'd begin to squirm. At first we thought it looked desperate—like the panicky wiggle of something stuck—and Ella insisted I help poke her back into the cage; but I sensed a higher design and told her to cool it. The hamster then released the bars and let loose in a freestyle shake, her arms stretched outward, her back arched, her upper and lower body swinging wildly in opposite directions. About two minutes later she had made it through, flopping to the ground and hustling on her way.

She was a risk-taker. One night I was awakened by faint but persistent scratching. It took me a while to discern where it was coming from, but there she was, halfway up the inside of the laundry hamper, dangling like some extreme-sports fanatic. Another time, after we hadn't seen her in a few days, I had started to wonder if she was gone for good. Then, as Ella was helping load the soap into the washing machine, out tumbled the hamster from the family-size box of detergent.

She was chalky white with soap dust. As Ella looked on, I wetted a cloth with warm water and wiped the hamster down. It felt like nursing a drug addict after an overdose. She trembled, stuck out her tiny tongue and vomited a greenish fluid. We were grossed out but fascinated. How did it get green? I worried that this was a prelude to her death and held her wrapped in a cloth on my lap for several hours. But she recovered and was back to scampering through the apartment by the end of the day.

Ted was in northern Africa laying down food-supply delivery routes for an expected famine. When he got back I brought him up to date on the hamster.

"Everything all right?" he said when I'd finished.

"Hunky-dory. Why?"

"What about that archaeological group? Weren't you supposed to go on a dig or something?"

I was, but I hadn't. I found I just couldn't get worked up enough over shards of ancient pottery. "It's on my list."

"So what else have you been up to?" he pursued. "Met anyone interesting lately?"

I had. Massimo. But I was hardly going to tell Ted about him. What Ted was really asking me, of course, was whether I was putting my luxury of free time to good use. The underlying question irked me because the implication, or at least the concern, was that I wasn't. That I was failing at constructive leisure. Instead of steeping myself in a new culture, coming home intellectually charged from museums, archaeological excursions or stimulating exchanges with other international types, I was whiling away my hours obsessing over a rodent.

I was thinking a lot about Massimo, too. He intrigued me in a way few people had. His focused lethargy, the gentle outrage he expressed for the world's disregard of smaller living things, his hazy virility. As I sipped my morning coffee or hung out the laundry on the balcony, I found myself imagining where he lived. I knew it was in the neighborhood—I'd seen him often enough walking his dog—but I didn't know where. What would his home look like? I'd only been in a few Italian apartments, most belonging to people who had lived abroad and were of an entirely different class from Massimo. With little to go on, I limited myself to his bedroom. Slowly I constructed Massimo's private space, adding or changing elements, eventually forming a full picture of a low-ceilinged boudoir with aquariums containing lizards, snakes and other drowsy reptiles lining one wall. Along another wall were tanks of tropical fish. I imagined a small gallery of nature photographs framed in black on the third wall: close-up, high-resolution shots of iguanas, turtles hatching or rare and exquisite burrowing animals. A few low, minimalist bookshelves held magazines and novels, perhaps *Moby Dick*, and tracts on ecology and animal life. Any traffic noise from outside was muted, and the interior soundtrack was only the soft gurgle of water and the light, moist panting of Massimo's German shepherd. His bed was in a corner, single but not austere. A bed that encapsulated his individuality, his aloneness, but that also signalled a certain vulnerability. A bed that, no matter how I fiddled with the configuration of his room, was always unmade.

My pretext for going back to the pet shop was to ask pertinent questions about beagles; really, I was just longing to share my hamster stories with Massimo. When I arrived he was standing behind the counter, staring downward in concentration as he spoke on the phone with someone about the fragility of turtles in transport. It was a balmy day and his mother had moved her chair nearer to the door. She gave me a stunted nod and shot her gaze away. I lingered by the bunny cage until Massimo finished his call.

"*Buon giorno, signora,*" he said, after he hung up.

I approached the counter and launched right into the hamster's clever escapes, her clothes-hamper escapade, her powdery brush with death. He listened, never quite laughing, but at times lifting his chin and broadening his smile enough to momentarily shed his woeful expression. When I finished he frowned thoughtfully.

"They're intelligent creatures," he said. "It's wrong when people don't take them as seriously as cats or dogs. Or people. They're smaller, but they don't matter less."

"Yes, I agree," I nodded. "They're just as important as us."

I began to time my walks home from teaching to coincide with Massimo's walks with his dog. I had an hour after work before I picked up Ella, so I loitered along the laneway, strolling casually up and down as if I were waiting for someone, which I was.

On the third day, he rounded the corner at a clip, the tension on the leash tight. He had a focused, athletic stride and his sad face had taken on a pained intelligence it didn't have in the pet shop. He stopped where the dog stopped to pee and leaned one arm against the wall, the other on his hip. I kept walking toward him, hoping he would look up. He did just before I reached him.

"*Signora,*" he nodded, a trace of a smile appearing on his lips.

"Hi."

His dog finished peeing and tugged on the leash. He yanked it lightly and the dog sat.

"Any news on when the beagles arrive?" I asked.

"Not for a while yet." He shook his head. "They're still too little. They still need their *mamma*." He said *mamma* with a shrug that was both helpless and full of yearning. I wondered about his relationship with his own strange mother, how he could stand the constant close proximity. I inquired how she was.

He shook his head tragically. "Not well. She's getting old and is becoming very nervous and making doubtful decisions. It's making life in the shop very difficult."

He explained that when he ordered animals, she would change the numbers without telling him. She had inexplicably lowered the prices on some products, raised them on others. She kept demanding to see the accounts and wouldn't give the books back when he needed to pay suppliers. Now she was threatening to bring in his uncle, who had left his job at the post office due to stress, to run the store with her.

"Perhaps she's just tired. Ready to retire," I suggested.

"If only!" he cried. "But she's too attached to the shop. She doesn't understand that if it weren't for my passion for it, it would have gone bankrupt by now. *Signora*, I have put seven years of my life into the store and those animals. It kills me to see her undoing my labor of love with this insanity."

He lowered himself to his knees and pressed his cheek against his dog's neck. Then he pulled his head back and a vague, blissful look passed between them. Again, an unexpected pang of longing swept over me.

A few days later, as I emerged from an afternoon nap, I came upon Sonia violently jabbing a broom into the corner behind a plant. When I approached she let out a scream and jumped back. The hamster sprang from the corner and darted behind the bookshelf.

Sonia was trembling. "*Signora*, it's not right you let it run around your home. This is a dirty animal. *Un ratto.*"

She insisted I come with her to Ella's room. There, she opened the armoire door and pointed. "You smell?" she said, making a face. "*Disgustoso.*"

She was right. The armoire did smell. I assured Sonia that I would deal with it; I was concerned she would quit. While the apartment was small and hardly needed a cleaning three times a week, the thought of losing Sonia was distressing. I'd come to rely on her. After she left, Ella and I got down on all fours and pulled out the toys and shoes and miscellaneous objects that had accumulated on the wardrobe floor. We discovered the source of the stink. A downy heap of chewed sock occupied the back corner of the wardrobe. It was the work of the hamster, of course. We pulled it out in small fistfuls; under it we discovered miniature mounds of her pellets. She'd made both a nest and toilet of Ella's closet.

This concerned me. In the past several weeks, the hamster had chewed into one of Ella's stuffed animals and eaten a hole through my favorite silk scarf. She was also keeping me awake at night by scratching the lining of our headboard. She was laying claim to territory that was not hers.

I phoned Massimo at the pet shop. Was it possible to potty train these creatures? He had talked, after all, of their intelligence.

"*Signora*," he said, after I explained what was happening, "you don't want to put her back in the cage?"

"How can I?" I said, surprised. "It would be different if she'd always been caged or if she weren't so smart. But you know how bright she is. And she's known freedom."

He sighed; he had problems of his own without being burdened with mine.

"How are things going with your mother?" I asked.

His candor was unexpected.

"*Terribile*. She's really become crazy." He lowered his voice. "We're trying to arrange for her to go live with my aunt in the countryside. Things are getting out of hand."

Putting inconvenient relations out to pasture? I thought Italians didn't do that sort of thing.

"She insists that my uncle be her partner and he's never even had a pet. Not so much as a goldfish. He calls hamsters guinea pigs, that's how much he knows."

"Couldn't you train him and all work there together?" I ventured. "Make it a family affair?"

"Never," he said. "It's him or me. I couldn't share my shop with a man like him."

"But if it's your shop, just say no."

"Yes, it's my shop. But my mother owns it."

"So it's her shop. She's the owner."

"No, it's mine. But she is the legal owner."

There was clearly some cultural nuance that I was failing to grasp, so I let it drop.

"So what's so wrong with your uncle?"

"He has no love for anything, least of all animals." Then Massimo added bitterly, "There are some things you can't teach."

"I suppose you're right," I replied, thinking of all the patience animals require, all the problems that can crop up. I thought of Sonia and the hamster. I thought about the beagle and wondered if I was really up to it. "Any news on the dogs?"

"Oh, yes!" His voice brightened. "They'll be in next week."

I still hadn't mentioned the puppy to Ted and Ella. Ted had left for Darfur and I had to admit the hamster was becoming a problem. I still admired her verve but I was sick of cleaning out tiny turds from under the kitchen appliances and the sink. And I could tell Sonia wouldn't hesitate to have another go at her, given the chance. Ella was beginning to make a few friends, and while she was devoted to the critter when she could show it off to her playmates, once the crowds decamped, her interest dissolved. If it weren't for all the cleaning up, both Ella and I might have forgotten she shared our apartment.

It struck me that a solution might be to move her outdoors. I could set up her cage on the balcony with some food and a litter area and a plastic tarpaulin to keep out the rain. I spent the afternoon making sketches of a few options, which I planned to take by the pet shop after I dropped Ella off at karate. On my way from the dojo I ran into Massimo in front of the *caffè* near his shop. He looked haunted.

"Massimo, are you all right?"

"I'm at my wits' end," he said in a scratchy whisper, looking around anxiously. "She found out I was looking to move her to my aunt's and now she refuses to talk to me. She's taken the pasta pots and the iron and the television and gone to stay at my uncle's. She's even accused me of stealing."

"Stealing? Stealing what?"

"Money from the store."

I insisted on buying him a drink and he followed me into the *caffè*. I ordered a glass of white wine but Massimo only wanted coffee.

"Can't you just show her the accounts?"

Massimo sighed. "Accounting in Italy is very complicated. We're so overtaxed that there are things one must do to avoid paying. Our system is very complex. Too complex."

"I see," I said. "Well, what's going to happen?"

"God only knows. My mother has a strong personality. Anything could happen." He glanced nervously toward the doorway.

I finished my wine. "Massimo, I wanted to talk to you about the dog. I'm concerned ... "

"Yes, I know," he nodded solemnly. Then he smiled such a tender, brave smile. "Please trust me. I will get you your dog."

When Ted returned from Africa I broke the news to him about the beagle. He was pulling on his jogging socks.

"Why?"

"Ella's been wanting one for ages."

"Yeah, so what? She's been wanting a horse and a pet monkey, too."

"Well, she's really wanted a dog. Anyhow, I've committed."

"I thought you hadn't told her yet."

"I haven't. I've committed to Massimo."

"Who the hell is Massimo?"

"The pet-shop guy."

"The serial killer? You've committed to the serial killer?"

He was trying to jolly me.

"He's actually a special guy."

"*Special*? Really."

"Unique."

Ted looked at me closely then shoved his foot into a shoe. "Why do you want a dog?"

I didn't know why. In fact, I was coming to the conclusion that I didn't want a dog. But I wanted something. When I finally spoke, my words sounded ridiculous—pitiable, even to me. "I want something to love."

Ted stared, dumbfounded. But he wasn't able to argue.

On the weekend we went to pick up the beagle while Ella was at karate, so we could surprise her. It was obvious Ted was coming along to make some territorial show with Massimo, to convey his distrust of him and his little animals and especially of his dealings with the susceptible children and mothers who fell under his spell. Another male had encroached upon his private realm and was screwing around with it and he didn't like it one bit.

Since our talk, Ted hadn't mentioned the dog, but he had talked about travelling less in the next while. About wanting us to go away for the weekend. Perhaps explore some Etruscan towns. But really, what would a few weekend excursions change? I wanted meaning and connection, and if a hamster or dog provided it, fine. I'd take it where I could get it.

When we got to the pet shop, it was the mother who stood behind the counter. Her hands grasped its edge for support, her spine curving like a smooth hill that peaked just below her shoulders.

"We're here to pick up our beagle," I explained. "Massimo and I agreed that I'd come by today to get it."

"Massimo's not here," she said, staring past me, her knee jerking up and down.

"When will he be back?"

"Try later."

"Later? When?"

"Try Monday."

"Monday? Aren't you closed Mondays?"

"Try later, then. I don't know."

"What about the dogs?" I asked. "Are they here?"

"You'll have to ask Massimo." Her eyes travelled over the containers of fish-care products lining the shelves to her left, while her hands fidgeted with a ring of keys.

Ted tried to pass off his relief with a light shrug. "Well, we tried. I guess we'll just have to come back later. Some other time." He headed to the exit.

Just as I turned to leave, a man emerged from the back of the shop. He had heavy bags under his eyes and hair slicked back into a ponytail. Massimo's mother shifted nervously out of his way. He slunk to the front window, grasping a small cardboard box. There, he reached in and pulled out a handful of baby hamsters and dumped them into the display cage.

The uncle.

Ted went to get Ella, and I headed straight for the laneway. It was earlier than Massimo's usual time for walking his dog, but I was frantic. I paced for about twenty minutes, careful not to step on the dog shit, before deciding to head back to the store. As I approached it I spotted Massimo, his arms loaded down with heavy sacks, his German shepherd at his side. They turned down a back alley.

"Massimo!" I cried, rushing toward him.

He stopped and turned. "*Signora*," he said, with his trademark forlorn look.

"Massimo, I was just at the shop!"

"Yes. It's over for me. The pet shop is finished."

I was anxious to find out what had happened, but he was straining under the weight of the sacks of premium dog food, and I insisted on helping take some of the load. I followed him down the alley, up a flight of stairs and into what turned out to be the apartment he and his mother shared above the pet shop.

Massimo unlocked the door, pushed it open and without a word we hauled the bags into a small, dark front hall. He stuck his head out the door then closed it and slid the safety chain across. Breathless from the hauling, he leaned his back against the door.

"What happened?" I asked at last.

He pressed a finger against his lips and pointed to the floor. "*Piano*. They can hear everything."

"Oh."

He frowned, avoiding my eyes. "I am sorry to say this," he whispered, "but the final straw was the dog."

"What dog?"

"Your beagle. It's gone. She gave it to someone else."

"What do you mean?"

"I told you, Mamma is a person with a difficult character. When she's convinced of something, no matter how crazy, she won't back down. She didn't think you were a suitable dog-owner."

"But I don't even know your mother." I laughed. "We've barely even spoken."

"Yes, I know. But she said she didn't trust you with a dog."

I couldn't believe what I was hearing—this kooky, spaced-out woman deemed me morally unfit to own a dog. Then I remembered hamster number one.

"Is this because of the hamster? The one my daughter squeezed too hard?"

"No, no," said Massimo, puzzled. "Hamsters die all the time, even if they're properly cared for. They're very fragile animals."

Why hadn't he told me this before?

"Then what?" I demanded. "What made her not trust me?"

"She doesn't want pets coming back. She was convinced that after a short time you would try to bring back the dog. She didn't trust you'd keep it."

"But that's … that's … "

"I know."

"But did you … ?"

Massimo looked mournfully into my eyes. "Of course, *signora*," he said. "Of course I trusted you. I insisted, but she would not listen. I insisted that pets were your life."

He then reached out and stroked my cheek lightly with the back of his hand and smiled that tender, intimate smile I'd witnessed so often as he gazed at his beloved creatures. The gaze that I'd quietly longed to have turned on me.

I needed some air.

As I slid the chain off the door, Massimo's dog pushed past me and nosed his way into an adjacent room. The door swung open enough for me to see inside: it was a bedroom, and on the wall were two posters, a faded one of a seventies rock band and another of a soccer player. In the corner was a single bed, made. Above it hung a framed drawing of the Madonna and child and on it a small stuffed kitten was propped against the pillow. Massimo's room.

That night in bed I turned to Ted and said, "This isn't working anymore."

"What isn't?" he asked.

"All of it. This whole package deal."

Ted was silent for a moment. Then he said, "What do you want to do? What do you want?"

"Out," I said. "I want out. Out of the house, out of being out of it. I want a real job. I can't do this lady-of-leisure thing."

Ted exhaled. "OK," he said, taking my hand. "We can start asking around. See if anyone has any leads."

"Let's do that."

Several weeks later I was unloading the dishwasher when the hamster appeared from beneath the refrigerator. She paused to nibble on a crumb. Without so much as a flicker of a forethought, I scooped her from the floor, carried her across the living room and stuck her in her cage. I took some extra telephone wire that had been stuffed in a kitchen drawer and wrapped it around the warped bars.

Ella was watching TV.

"Let's go out for an ice cream," I said.

"OK."

I moved towards the door.

"Why are you taking the cage?" Ella asked.

"We're setting her free."

"No!"

"Yes."

"Where?"

"In the park."

"But she could die! She could be eaten by a hawk or something."

"Perhaps. But she's tough."

Ella considered. She didn't have a leg to stand on. She hadn't looked at the hamster in weeks.

"OK. But only if I can get a rabbit."

"Forget it."

She huffed and then sighed.

"Let's go," I said.

We set the hamster free by a bunch of shrubs at the edge of a woody area. I pulled her out of the cage and gave her fur one last stroke. As I ran my finger down her back, she swung around, sank her tiny teeth into my hand, and then took off into the shrubs.

"Ouch!" I cried.

"I guess she was sick of you," said Ella.

"I guess so."

On the way back we stopped in front of the pet shop, which was closed, and left the empty cage against the door. Then, hand in hand, we went for ice cream.

The Girls in Bikinis

FOR THE PAST FOURTEEN YEARS I've worked as a civil servant, most recently with Foreign Affairs. The civil service is not renowned for its risk-takers and I am not one. I like to think my fortes have been steady work, efficiency and a certain critical perspective. When I applied for the Rome position I understood that it was an exceedingly *long* long shot. Rome is a reward posting, where diplomats get sent after putting in time in places like Chad or Latvia, or it's where they're put out to pasture after the pressure cookers of the Middle East or China. Italy's a second-tier country in political importance; first-tier in luxury. A posting few get offered and none say no to, least of all a mid-level manager toiling in the stultifying bureaucracy of Ottawa.

But I was a coward or, as Gwen put it, a weasel. I didn't tell her about the offer, and by the time I'd made up my mind, we had less than a month left together. Understandably, she was more than a little upset.

Gwen and I had been together for a decade. I'd come out a couple of years earlier with a woman whom, shortly after we'd moved in together, I found naked on our futon with our landlady. When I met Gwen, she didn't strike me as someone capable of breaking another person's heart, which was immensely appealing. She was eager to be with me—not in an excitable adolescent way—but in how she put her full self into our encounters. During our fourth or fifth conversation, Gwen told me she didn't want to waste any more time; it was clear that we'd make very compatible partners. She wanted to know then, that night, if I was in or out. I considered my options: returning alone to my studio apartment, which was clean and pleasant but had always felt temporary, or moving in with a woman whose presence was like a hearth, enshrouding me in warmth and reassurance.

We did make very compatible partners at first. You might say Gwen and I were a champion domestic tag team, with Gwen leading the charge. We shared an affection for animals and adopted a couple of mutts from the pound the week I moved into her farmhouse just outside Ottawa. Gwen covered the morning walk; I did the p.m. Weekends we formed a twelve-legged power-walking foursome, leaving the house by 7:30 a.m. so we could get on with our day early. We had a garden, which I tended and Gwen cooked from. With a group of like-minded neighbours we spearheaded a campaign to stop the burning of toxic waste in the local hospital incinerator. We strove to live in a way that reflected our values, to be good—and also accountable. I recall, for instance, a long discussion about how grungy a plastic bag had to get before we felt justified in recycling it rather than rinsing and reusing it. (We agreed that four times seemed right.) At night I would lie in bed going over the convergences:

See all that we have in common? See why this union makes such sense? And yet.

And yet, despite our deep sense of responsibility for the state of the world, I couldn't help but notice as our private habits slid more and more toward seeking comfort. Meals and snacks and treats took on expanding importance. In a covert effort to add spice to our life, Gwen spent weekends preparing exotic dishes. One week Thailand, the next West Africa, then Chile. Or why not a banquet-sized spread of soul food from the American South? Why not, indeed. The food was invariably heavy on sauces and kept us in leftovers for days. And yet it wasn't enough, for either of us. After we had heartily acknowledged the peoples of the world with our main course, we'd bring out crème brûlée or chocolate mousse or, more often than not, ice cream, instant pudding or some other whipped, creamed or pulverized dessert and hunker down in front of a TV documentary. As long as we weren't polluting our minds with a lowbrow sitcom we could indulge in edible junk. Neither of us breathed a word about how fat we were getting.

We were loving—our friends all used that word, *loving*—and we hugged in a way I can only describe as compulsive. I once kept track of how many times we hugged in a sixteen-hour period: twenty-eight. And yet, the arguments! We bickered about which way the plates should face in the dishwasher (followed by a big hug); whether the British or Americans had caused more death and destruction worldwide (then shared a peacemaking embrace); who had farted (followed by a wave of the hand and a quick squeeze).

But even we weren't fooled. We began seeing a couples therapist, a woman who was just as heavy and humorless as Gwen and I had become. She suggested we had a communication problem. Gwen agreed but I balked. All we did, between hugging and eating, was dialogue, process, confess and re-evaluate. I was tired of it. I said I wanted to be left alone with some of my thoughts, although what I truly wanted was to be left alone. Then Gwen brought up the Big Unspoken: a sex life that had died barely after a pulse had been established. The therapist urged us to think outside the box. When I pointed out that we hadn't gone anywhere near our boxes in ages, she flashed me a schoolmarm look.

But even then: right move. We signed up for a sex seminar at the local queer bookstore and learned about techniques to "liven our libidos," from flirting to fisting. We returned home with a bag full of gadgets, gear and lotions, but with the all-round forced gaiety, who were we kidding? We were a couple of forty-plus, overweight, dog-loving civil servants, not hot young dykes keen to push the outer limits. Having to strap on an ebony dildo, which Gwen took to calling Kunta Kinte in an effort to make it feel like a romp, was the last straw. I put the stuff in a shoebox and shoved it in the closet under a pile of clothes earmarked for the women's shelter. Relieved, we went back to cuddling.

Not long afterward, over breakfast, Gwen proposed. She'd made toast and a pot of herbal tea and had laid out little jars of homemade jam. I looked at the tea and the toast and the jam, and then at Gwen's strained, eager face—a face that projected nothing but love and the desire to be loved back— and made my decision: I was going to Rome. Alone. I cared about Gwen but I could no longer take not loving her the way she loved me.

So when I stepped off the plane at Fiumicino airport a month later, it was with immense relief. The summer sun assaulted the tarmac, turning everything in view into a pulsating plane of white. But it was the scent—the hint of a creamy flower in full, aching bloom—that confirmed exactly what needed confirming: This was *not* home. Change might be possible. And this was my chance. I made my way through customs, pushed into a cab, then stumbled into the hotel lobby. In a small, dark, air-conditioned room I slept and forgot.

It was six-thirty when I hauled myself out of bed. The room was aglow with the warm apricot light of late afternoon. I pushed open the window and the smell of simmering sweet peppers and tomatoes floated in, along with the din of voices mingling below. I showered, changed and stepped out into my first Roman evening.

It was a weekday but the piazza was pulsating with life. People of all ages were all rambling with arms looped through elbows or wrapped around shoulders, chattering and calling to one another. They paused to throw their chin up in a laugh or to lean forward, shaking a cusped hand to make a point. The young women seemed to have confused reality with an MTV video: clunky gold crosses dangled between their brown breasts and lacy thongs rose from between bum cheeks that their jeans barely covered. And the older women! In Canada they would have passed for hookers with considerable work experience. Who knew sparkly jewelry could be worn against crinkly cleavage with such nonchalance? Even the older men were shamelessly flashy— natty and cologned, sporting pressed shirts and trendy eyewear, puffing on cigarettes with satisfaction. There wasn't another soul in sight in a cotton leisure suit and comfortable shoes.

What really caught my eye, though, was the way they ate ice cream—cones piled high with chocolate, pistachio and hazelnut under a cloud of whipped cream. I couldn't detect a flash of guilt or greed. These people ate ice cream as if they'd be pleased to pass their cone around and let everyone have a taste—and if it came back with only one bite left for them, that would be just fine. They acted as if the utterly amazing innovation of taste, texture, temperature and color that they balanced lightly between their fingers and tongued into their mouths was nothing but a delicious snack, a passing pleasure, something to enjoy and move on from, not a desperately relied-upon taste sensation that kept them buoyed above the abyss of depression and anxiety. I wanted to be able to eat ice cream like that. I also wanted to look a little more like them while eating ice cream. Walking through streets full of half-naked sexpots, I suddenly felt like an overstuffed, badly upholstered couch. I wasn't planning on exposing my navel in this lifetime, but it dawned on me that I might branch out beyond beige cotton durables.

The embassy found me a small apartment on the edge of Villa Pamphilij, a vast, undulating park with paths named after famous women. I decided it was now or never: I would take up jogging. The move was akin to volunteering as a subject for research on torture—it was August and still thirty degrees Celcius at sundown—but I had no option. The only gym in my neighborhood was closed for the month so its staff could vacation. Gradually, I built up my evening sessions around the park. I'd start with a slow trot up Viale Sorelle Brontë, then hang a right on Via Florence Nightingale and hoof it along Viale dei Curie. After a month I was running circles around Rosa Luxemburg.

Then my exercise routine got an unexpected boost. In mid-October, when Romans finally get serious about summer wrapping up, the ambassador held a dinner for a few embassy staffers and Italians of various professions. I was seated beside an art historian in her early fifties. Her name was Oriana and she was a dead ringer for Grace Kelly: the perfect posture, a pastel twin-set and honeyed hair sculpted into a perfect wave. Once we got past the formalities—namely, me telling her about my impressions of Italy and how much I was delighting in the food—she turned out to be interesting. She was an expert in baroque painting and was in the midst of organizing an exhibit of work by a seventeenth-century female artist I'd never heard of. I told her about my evening exercise in Villa Pamphilij on the paths named after famous women. Her eyes lit up: she loved the park and walked her dog there every morning. It turned out that Oriana and I lived in the same condominium complex.

Apologizing profusely, Oriana left soon after dessert was served, saying she had another engagement she had to attend. As we said our goodbyes her eyes flickered hesitantly, then she slipped her hand into her purse, pulled out her card and gave it to me. She had an exercise room in her apartment, she said. Would I be interested in joining a small group of her friends for an aerobics class?

As flattered as I was by Oriana's misreading of me as a fitness buff, I was philosophically opposed to aerobics. Physically opposed too. Aerobics looked both hard and dumb. Still, it was a chance to meet people. My social life up to that point had consisted of lunches and after-work drinks with fellow Canadians from the embassy—until the ambassador had confided that he felt the staff had adapted far too well to Italy. Lunch networking meetings were stretching for hours and too much laughter was filtering up to his domain. He told me to get things back on track. I did; I monitored the breaks and got on people's cases if they looked like they were having too much fun. There were two immediate upshots: the lunch breaks got shorter and my colleagues began to quietly despise me. Friendly banter with Vinicio, the twenty-year-old barman with sculpted facial hair who made my cappuccino every morning, was as close as I got to friendship.

Aerobics classes were twice a week. I'd buzz and be let into the grandiose foyer by Olga, Oriana's enormous Ukrainian maid, who was dressed in a ridiculous French maid get-up, including a frilly white apron.

It was right out of a Fred and Ginger flick. The marble floor was so glossy I nearly landed on my ass the first time over it. Bookshelves lined the hall, holding volumes and volumes of art books likely worth more than my life savings. An ancient Roman bust that seemed real—what did I know?—was spotlit in an alcove. Olga escorted me past the living room, which was overwhelmed by lugubrious still-life paintings. The walls and sofas were spotless white, and corner shelves displayed reconstructed Etruscan vases. The decor was a stilted combo of minimalist modern and ornate ancient, with a whopping dose of self-celebration. On every surface not occupied by archaeological treasures were large silver-framed photographs of Oriana, her husband and her daughter posing their way through vacations at the seaside, in the mountains and in European capitals, where fountains shimmered in the background. I thought of the picture that had sat on my father's teak desk in our suburban Ottawa home since 1970, the lone remnant of our one family trip to the department store photographer. My relatively happy childhood suddenly seemed shamefully deprived.

There were six of us in the class, including Oriana and the instructor, Giorgina. There was something pouty and overfed about them—like geese on their way to becoming foie gras. They moved with a resigned, drawling elegance. Most had been friends of Oriana since childhood. They were all around fifty and still in their prime—with the kind of looks that come from regular visits to the hairdresser, live-in domestic help, seasonal vacations and a whole lot of money.

The first night, I showed up in baggy sweat pants and my comfy old *Stop Burning Toxic Waste Now!* T-shirt. They wore form-fitting aerobics wear in smoky European colors and cashmere sweaters they'd cast off as they warmed up. Only the perennially leather-skinned and snooty Patrizia twitched an eyebrow disapprovingly at my get-up; the others were too discreet. But compared to their workout chic I looked as if I'd just rolled off a turnip truck.

They always smiled and said the hello and goodbye *ciaos*. But after a few weeks of exercising my basic Italian it became clear that I was off their grid—a bizarre combination of embassy prestige, aesthetic ineptitude and other things I couldn't even begin to fathom. I doubt they suspected I was gay; I don't think they would have acted so casually had they harbored that suspicion.

I kept expecting that sooner or later we'd settle into casual workout patter. This was Italy, land of the loud and friendly. Apart from the greetings, though, they ignored me. Even Giorgina usually overlooked me when she checked back alignments during our abs exercises, which was irritating. But being irrelevant meant I didn't have to bother. I could just watch. And while these women embodied everything I was not and had no desire to be, I found them captivating.

Mostly I watched Giorgina watch herself. She was all showgirl wiggles and winks. She strove for cuteness, a goal I found idiotic, and she achieved it with flying colors. She had a small, muscular body with a notable boob job and high round cheekbones to match. A tiny patch of sweat collected just above the crack of her bum and even that managed to look winsome. While she led our workout she'd sometimes crinkle her nose at herself in the mirror and drop one shoulder. Once, while she had us shaking our hips to a Latin beat, she trailed her tongue along her lips. I snorted—I couldn't help it—but she just winked, threw her head back and gave her hips an extra squirm, pleased by her cheesy performance.

These were professional women—a biologist, a translator, an economics professor and Oriana, the art historian—but they didn't have the frenzied, beleaguered look of the high-powered working mothers I knew. No doubt they'd worked hard to get where they were—this was male-dominated Italy after all. But they'd somehow slipped their jobs comfortably in among managing their homes and the lives of husbands and children, ski vacations, summers at the beach and looking gorgeous.

Sometimes Oriana's daughter, Flaminia, would come in. She was tall and blond and had eyebrows like the wings of a crow. She wasn't pretty—her young face couldn't carry her aquiline nose—but she glowed like the pampered and prized fourteen-year-old girl she was. She would pause to watch us for a moment with a blank, lofty expression. Then she'd cross the room and wrap her arms around Oriana from behind. This was mother-daughter interaction from another planet. At that age I remember maintaining a well-defined physical distance between me and my parents and being mortified if any part of my body happened to accidentally brush theirs. Even as an adult there was always some awkward positioning before the peck on the cheek at the end of a visit. Oriana and Flaminia rubbed cheeks and practically cooed.

On the back wall of the aerobics room hung a large framed poster reproduction of a Roman or perhaps Greek fresco or mosaic of two young women, one holding a pair of small weights and the other, with bracelets around her wrists and forearms, poised to release a discus. The girls were muscular, round-bellied, triumphant. And wearing bikinis. Red ones. The one lifting a discus high above her head was the spitting image of Flaminia.

As culturally fascinating as the aerobics classes were, they weren't pumping out friendships. I was lonely. With Gwen I hadn't needed to make an effort. She usually did all the inviting and organizing, which I was happy not to deal with. When I had arrived in Rome I'd sent a bunch of emails and cards inviting friends from Ottawa to come visit, but only a few people had responded, noncommittally. I'd assumed they were frosty because I'd walked out on Gwen, but now I was beginning to question if I really had any friends.

Solitude filled all my non-working hours. On my lunch break I'd take a book and a slice of pizza or a gelato (or both) and sit on a park bench near the embassy. One day I looked up from the guide to Roman gods and goddesses I was reading and noted a middle-aged couple necking on the edge of a nearby fountain. This in itself was unremarkable. Roman parks in the afternoon were cuckold central. Benches practically writhed with straight couples of all ages going at it like teenagers dying to get past first base before their parents walked in. The male half of this particular couple had one long leg wrapped around the woman, gamely pinning her to the marble. His tie was thrown over his shoulder and his pant leg was bunched around his knee.

When they came up for air, my heart did a *tha-dump*. It was Giorgina, the aerobics instructor.

"Giorgina!" I called out.

In my amazement at having bumped into someone I knew, I had failed to think. Giorgina was married and had a son. In fact, I'd briefly met her husband when he had picked her up after an aerobics class. A short, balding, reptilian man with a grinding handshake. Not the man by the fountain with a mop of greying curls and orange lipstick smeared around his mouth.

Giorgina fumbled in a jacket pocket and pulled out a pair of glasses. She stuck them on, squinted and sighed impatiently.

"*Ah no, va bene,*" I could hear her say. *No, it's all right. It's just an American I know.* She then said something else that I couldn't make out and they both stood up. She made a rolling motion with her hand to indicate to me that she was in a hurry, then she and her man hastened off across the park.

It seemed Miss Cha-cha-cha had more than one dance partner.

At the next aerobics class Giorgina was particularly fired-up. No mamboing that night; she had us down on the floor performing excruciating leg exercises. "You must imagine you are squeezing a five-hundred-euro bill between your thighs!" she ordered, and when she thought we weren't pressing hard enough she put her hands on her hips, leaned forward and yelled that it was now one thousand euros. "*Forza, signore!* I want to see your thighs tremble!" she screamed, and our legs quaked.

As we segued into thigh presses, back stretches and air bicycles, the women chatted about their lives. They had maids and mothers and husbands and lovers and one or two children and dogs and they talked about them all in the same lightly helpless and derisive tone. "When Antonio and I were still in love … " or "I haven't been able to sleep in a week because of Mario's snoring. Thank God he's in Milan this week; his mistress will have to put up with it." Then they'd share a raised eyebrow. Were they serious? I hadn't a clue. Or they'd talk about a piece of jewellery that had gone missing and drop their voices so Olga wouldn't hear. "Have you checked her room? Send her out to get flowers or bread and search her room." Or they'd tell about a friend's daughter who had been diagnosed with a horrible, crippling disease and shake their heads fatalistically, say "*facciamo le corna*" and make the sign with their fingers that could mean someone had been cuckolded, but in this case warded off evil.

Sometimes, near the end of the class, Oriana's husband Cesare would come home from work. He was an older, moustached gentleman who brought to mind Omar Sharif. A man my grandmother would have described as dashing or gallant and whom I would describe as unctuous. He always approached crying "*Buona sera, belle signore!*" and beaming with his immense white teeth while a whiff of his after-shave floated over our gathering of lovely ladies. Oriana, bum in the air or legs pumping, would turn and beam back. The others kept working out without any awkwardness or forced friendliness. They didn't pay Cesare much attention, but they didn't mind being admired.

Their benevolent indifference toward Cesare intrigued me. If they'd been wealthy Ottawa matrons I'd have long since quit the class. Desperate as I was for company, spending two hours a week moving my limbs to pop music with a bunch of rich married women who ignored me wasn't my idea of a good time. But no Ottawa matrons I knew accomplished womanhood the way this little group did. Gwen's older sister Marjorie, a lawyer with three kids, married to a member of Parliament, was their Canadian equivalent. Yet with Marjorie there was always an underlying tension, a fear playing on her forehead that despite the millions of things she did in a day to prove how useful she was to everyone, she still wasn't deserving. Marjorie knew she doubted her own worth and it made her resentful as hell. But with these women I couldn't detect a smidgen of doubt. They were worth every thousand-euro bill they imagined squeezing between their thighs, and a whole lot more.

As I was leaving aerobics that night, Giorgina timed her exit to mine.

"Colleen-a," she said, pronouncing my name like the Italian word for hill, *collina*. "I would like to explain about the park."

"Oh please."

Giorgina looked on the verge of tears. "I must explain. I am in such a state of confusion. You could call it a crisis. Yes, a real crisis."

And then she burst out crying. A little girl's bawl. She grasped the floppy collar of my after-workout fleece and pressed her head against my shoulder and boo-hoo-hooed. Just as quickly she straightened up and dabbed her eyes with a tissue that appeared out of nowhere.

"I'm so sorry," she said. "It's just that, you see, my husband, Pierangelo, is a judge. You understand what that means, no?"

"I know what a judge is."

"Yes, of course you do," she smiled. "But what I mean is that he is a very important man in Italy. *Molto importante.*"

She puffed out a breath. "And because of this, he is never at home. *Mai.* Never. Not even on the weekends. Not even for Sunday lunch. *Mai, mai, mai.* Work is his life."

"A workaholic," I offered.

Giorgina's eyebrows pressed together. "Maybe, I don't know. But you see how I find myself? It is not possible. A woman needs *amore, affetto,* no? And Gianluca, well, you saw him, no?" She grinned and rolled her eyes up and let out a "ha!"

It was time to speed up the conversation. "I won't tell anyone, Giorgina, if that's what you're worried about."

"Ah, yes. You are right," she said, as if I was the one worried about word of her liaison spreading. "No one must know." She gave my hand a gentle squeeze and turned to go.

Giorgina's overwhelming frivolity hadn't bothered me until now; she was my aerobics instructor after all, not my financial advisor. But I resented her assuming she could blow me off with tears and charm.

"I'm sure you've thought of it," I said, "but cheating isn't exactly the best way to improve a marriage."

She turned back to me. "Maybe not, no … "

"So why don't you address the issues. Talk to him."

"Oh, but I have. I have told him many times that he must work less."

"I mean about your 'crisis.'"

"Oh, never! What could I possibly say?"

A few suggestions came to mind, but I resisted.

"If it's that tough to talk, why not get some help—a counsellor or therapist or whatever they call them here?" I was the last person to promote couples counselling, but my urge to quash Giorgina's smugness was on auto-drive. "Professional help."

Giorgina just smiled, with a hint of what might have been pity. "Colleen-a, you are very … " She clenched her delicate fist and shook it. " … very *decent*. I like Americans very much. I have good friends in Connecticut. They are just like you, very nice, but how do you say? Simple? Yes, simple. Every week they go to their counsellor and talk, talk, talk."

"Better than cheating, don't you think?"

Giorgina was unfazed. "Yes, of course. But between a husband and a wife, too much honesty can be a weight, no? *Heavy.* A husband is not a friend, no? He's a husband."

"I honestly wouldn't know."

"Yes," she nodded, "that's right. You are *nubile*."

She glanced at her watch. "*O, mio Dio!*" Then she hesitated, the same hesitation that had passed through Oriana before she'd handed me her card the night of the ambassador's dinner. An upper-class hesitation—a surrender to the impulse to be spontaneous followed by an immediate tug of regret.

She kissed me. On both cheeks. And fled.

Nubile, I learned when I got home and looked it up, meant "single," a status I had chosen. But what had begun as intoxicated relief to be on my own had slowly transformed into a total-body ache for human contact. I'd even begun thinking about Gwen. I found myself entertaining little fantasies about the two of us exploring the open-air food markets or meeting up for an *aperitivo* in some historic piazza after work. Or Gwen cooking up a storm of Italian food—and me eating it. They were scenarios full of the old comfort and habits that, frankly, depressed me. I hadn't heard from Gwen—she was being stoically silent, thank God—but I knew her well enough to know that despite her anger, she'd join me at the drop of a hat. And that kept me from calling.

A stack of gay listings had been sitting on my kitchen table for weeks. I finally gave them a serious look. On the last Sunday of every month there was a women's night in what was once Rome's central slaughterhouse. I was more in the market for friendship than meat, but it was time to find someone I could actually relate to.

I should have headed home as soon as I saw the crowd spreading in front of warehouses along the dimly lit side street. Instead, I stood my ground in the lineup, jostled by women with oversized belt buckles and too much hair gel, fretting as only a Canadian could about my exact spot in line. Very far back, it turned out. Every ten minutes or so a virago in a tank top cruised the lineup and ushered her choices through the entrance like beauty pageant contestants who'd made the cut. Sometimes she seemed to know the women she let in, sometimes she just seemed to approve of how they looked. This was pissing me off, and by the time I had paid the outrageous entrance fee and had my wrist stamped—almost two hours later—I was fuming.

I realized immediately that any hope for an exchange of Sapphic pleasantries had been foolhardy. The violently pounding music precluded talk. I squeezed toward the bar to get a beer and, rodent-like, followed the wall to a corner observation point. Despite my rotten mood I tried to look open and approachable, and apparently failed. Everyone had shown up with friends, pressed together in groups and pairs, their social and sexual needs taken care of. I wasn't spared more than a passing glance.

As I inched my way back around the bar toward the exit, I noticed a staircase up to a balcony overlooking the dance floor. Mingling in the ample space were women of a certain age (mine), surrounded by a bevy of sexy young things in tank tops, metallic glints in their navels. An older woman with spiky dark hair and a suit jacket stood out; there was something commanding in her stance. She stood nodding into her cellphone while scanning the *profanum vulgus* below like Hestia guarding her Vestal Virgins. To my surprise she looked my way. I held her gaze, hoping she'd interpret it as a bold dare and not the puppy-dog yearning of someone so desperate for company she could howl.

Hestia kept my gaze, but instead of smiling or nodding she reached out and imperiously pulled a buffed Virgin into her fold. The bitch. I'd had enough and availed myself of that versatile hand sign I'd learned from the aerobics ladies.

It packed more punch than I'd anticipated. Her face twisted into a frightening sneer and she came ploughing down the stairs toward me. This wasn't the moment to put my conflict resolution training into practice. I shoved my way out the back exit and ran down the darkened street as fast as my legs would carry me. Which, despite having taken up jogging a mere six months earlier, was fast enough to leave Hestia in the dust.

I decided that reading was about as much excitement as I wanted for a while. My selections had evolved from guidebooks to historical mysteries to serious novels set in the ancient world. The highlight so far was Marguerite Yourcenar's fictional diary of Hadrian, one of the last great Roman emperors. Yourcenar had spent years researching Hadrian's life and wandering the sprawling ruins of his villa near Rome. I'd never been a romantic, but standing among the crumbling palace walls and cypress trees with her book in hand I felt like I could almost touch the past.

It was the depraved and cruel emperor Nero, though, whom I had to thank for my change in fortune. One Saturday afternoon in March after I had visited the spooky remains of Domus Aurea—Nero's extravagant villa—I stopped by a little outdoor caffè on the Colle Oppio, the slope of land overlooking the Coliseum. All the tables were taken, but when I glanced around for a place to sit a woman pulled back an empty chair at her table and motioned me over. Later she told me she knew instantly I was a foreigner because I was having a cappuccino after lunch, which Italians consider a culinary crime—something about milk being too hard to digest at the end of a meal. Whatever.

She introduced herself as Martina. She had a broad, tanned face, eyes shielded by black sunglasses and short-cropped hair dyed out of the tube most Italian hairdressers seemed to use—an intense chocolate brown that flamed to copper in the sunshine. Her mouth was wide and sensual, curving up at the corners like a crocodile's. She was shortish and broad-shouldered and emitted casual authority.

Martina sat drinking espresso with Livia, an exuberant woman in her sixties who worked in a bakeshop and lived in Martina's apartment building. Livia wore thick, gold hoop earrings and gold necklaces and had some kind of sparkle gel spread across her eyelids. When I told them I was from Canada, Livia cried "O Dio santo!" and told me about her brother who lived in Hamilton. She wanted to hear about Niagara Falls, the legendary, endless underground malls and stories of extreme cold. With Martina looking on with a bemused smile, I put my sketchy Italian to work, pulling out tales of minus-thirty-degree weather and the old childhood chestnut of tongue sticking to cold metal. Livia clapped her hands and slapped her knees and made exclamatory noises.

Then she insisted I join them for dinner, and before I knew it the three of us were crammed into Livia's 1965 Cinquecento, bumping across Rome to a pizzeria in Testaccio, a working-class neighborhood not far from the slaughter-house-cum-venue-of-lesbian-posing. As we moved through the Roman traffic, seventies pop icon Mina shook the speakers, belting out her heartbreak. Martina smoked and swerved and honked and made obscene hand gestures and joked with Livia, who prattled in machine-gun Italian beside her.

Over pizza I learned that Martina was a cop. She worked for the Guardia di Finanza, the police force that investigated tax evasion and financial corruption. After dinner the three of us walked the five minutes from the restaurant to their building for a grappa nightcap.

Martina led the way upstairs, the muscles of her calves swelling and receding. When we got to her door, Livia clasped my arm and pressed her cheek against mine. "The wee hours are made for wee ones like you. Goodnight." She pointed a finger at Martina and said "*Mi raccomando!*"—Be good!—then continued up the stairs.

Martina took out her keys and opened the door. Her arm reached out to close it and it hit me that I wasn't in the market for friendship at all. I desperately needed to get laid. I reached out, slid my hand around the back of her neck and pulled her mouth to mine.

The next morning as I lay tangled in her sheets Martina tossed me a helmet and told me she'd give me a lift home on her way to work. Outside on the street she introduced me to her Ducati Monster. It was black and "nay-keda"—naked—Martina explained with a grin, all the tubes and works exposed. Even for someone as unimpressed by vehicles as I am, sitting on the back of the motorcycle was a dream. I had a new and unexpected appreciation for the phrase "sex on wheels."

We tore through Rome, Martina treating red lights like suggestions from someone whose judgment she didn't trust. We roared along Via della Conciliazione towards Saint Peter's Basilica and swerved back along the Tiber. I held Martina's hips and leaned back, letting the wind, as hot as a hairdryer, whip over my skin. When we arrived I climbed off. Delirious.

Martina gave me a last, full-on kiss goodbye.

Reluctantly I walked down the sidewalk and unlocked the iron gate that led into the courtyard of my condominium complex. As I pushed it open I heard the Ducati purring behind me.

"You live here?" Martina called from the road. I turned and saw her straddling the motorcycle with an odd, troubled expression. "In this condominium here?"

Was I missing something? Did she think I'd used her, slummed it with a cop for kicks before returning to my luxurious pad? "The embassy found it for me. Do you want to come up?"

"No, no." Martina shook her head. "Do you know any of your neighbors?"

I mentioned Oriana and the aerobics. Martina just nodded.

"Are you sure you don't want to come up?" I asked again.

But again she shook her head. Then she blew me a kiss and promised to call.

She didn't. Not the next day and not the next week. I called her a mere twenty times a day at first, but neither she nor an answering machine picked up. Feeling both lascivious and pitiful, I even set out one night with a map to find her apartment and loitered outside her place for longer than I care to reveal. The fact was sex with Martina had been a whole new can of spaghetti. With Gwen, making love had been a slow-paced, frustrated trudge toward climax. But Martina made love the way she lit a cigarette or drove her Ducati: with an economy of movement, a transparency of intention. Easily and gracefully and to great effect. But I'd been naive to assume that just because I was keen to bond with Martina, she was keen to bond with me. For all I knew she slept with a new foreigner each week—spent her free time cruising Rome for lone, pale-skinned, short-haired women drinking cappuccinos after lunch.

When the phone finally rang, it was Livia. I tried, but couldn't hide my disappointment. "I'm sorry it's not Martina," she said, "but trust me, forget about her. She can't help how she acts. Come with me to the beach."

My experience of waterfront recreation was limited to Ontario cottaging, where a lake was considered over-populated if you could see more than a couple of cottages from your dock. On the Fregene beach outside Rome you were lucky to claim a foot beyond your towel. Every inch of sand was taken up with glistening human flesh. I felt like a newcomer in some hedonistic rave; a family-friendly orgy where as long as you were nearly naked and oblivious to the most basic safety rules, you'd get along just fine.

Livia peeled down to her leopard-print bikini and her ropes of shiny necklaces. She adored the sun, she told me, and spent every day off from May to October roasting. I thought of how Gwen and I used to spread sunscreen on any exposed body parts even to take the dogs for a walk. Here babies waddled naked and sunscreen-free in the froth of the tide. I scanned the beach for an anxious face and couldn't even spot a lifeguard. Given how engrossed the adults were in their cellphone conversations, this should have been worrisome, but somehow it wasn't.

Livia and I ate hunks of watermelon, drank from glistening green bottles of mineral water and talked about our lives. I told her about my work troubles. And my feelings of guilt around Gwen. She told me about her husband dying when she was only twenty-three and how she'd raised, alone, the son of a friend who had become addicted to heroin. How she had been a lifelong Communist and how she still attended every protest march she could, because it was the next best thing to a party. How if all the lies the nuns had told her growing up turned out to be true, and heaven and hell really existed, she hoped heaven was just like Cuba, with samba music and endless beaches. Then she leaned back, her short, brown legs flopped open and she fell asleep.

From under my baseball cap, I spied teenage couples furtively feeling each other up and mothers smoking and gossiping and whacking their kids' bare bums if they kicked up sand or dropped their ice cream cone. I watched the slouched fathers, depleted and trapped by all the family togetherness. I watched girls with small, hard breasts run topless without anyone batting an eye, and the grandmothers, creased and saggy in their bikinis, reading Agatha Christie paperbacks with bright yellow covers, unfazed by the chaos around them. Back and forth sinewy men with sun-baked skin paced the beach selling creamy slices of coconut from pale-blue buckets, crying "*Cocco bello!*"

And I noticed I was the only woman on the beach in a one-piece bathing suit. I'd brought my Speedo from Ottawa, and although it had tenfold the fabric of any other suit on the beach, it left me feeling exposed. I felt like some relic from the Victorian past who'd washed up on the shore. Next to my jewellery-laden, leather-skinned, Communist friend, all that was missing to complete my look was a face-shading bonnet and bloomers.

Finally I lay back, closed my eyes and gave myself over to the sun, as if making up for a lifetime buried in winter. On the beach with Livia I felt some of my insulation melt away; nerves I didn't know I had began to prickle.

In August Livia invited me to go with her to Sicily and I gratefully accepted. Along with hordes of vacationing Italians we squeezed onto a ferry that took us down the coast from Civitavecchia to Palermo. From there we bused to the beach, where we remained for two weeks, Livia eagerly initiating me into the art of laziness. We stayed in a small, no-frills *pensione* (breakfast included: *caffè latte* and a fat, oozing brioche). In the morning we lay on the beach. Then we'd collapse after a lunch of fish or *una Caprese*—tomatoes and fresh mozzarella— and sleep through the crushing heat of the afternoon. We'd re-emerge for a couple more hours of beach before dinner. Our biggest challenge was digesting.

Part of our morning beach routine was reading the Italian papers. I usually just scanned the headlines to keep pace with the never-ending political scandals. But one morning a half-page article in the business section caught my eye: the CEO of a large insurance company was under investigation for bribing a judge to secure the purchase of another company. Hardly news in Italy, but I recognized the man in the photo: Cesare, Oriana's husband. Martina's caginess when she dropped me off at my apartment finally made sense. She must have been working on the case.

Near the end of our stay I cajoled Livia into taking a break from doing nothing to come with me on a day trip. I'd been reading about Villa Romana del Casale, a gem of a fourth-century residence that had been covered by a mudslide and not rediscovered until the 1800s; as a result, all the decorative detail was preserved.

We took an early-morning bus, winding past quaint hilltop towns. Livia, despite agreeing to come, was grumpy about the long ride. She kept shaking her head and pointing out crude, half-finished cinder-block constructions. "Mafia urban planning. *Bello, no?*"

When we reached our destination we followed the crowd under the punishing sun into the covered ruins. I was completely unprepared for what awaited us. Every room— and there were dozens of them—was covered in elaborate, exquisitely detailed mosaics: wild beasts tearing apart antelopes, spears thrust into lions, enormous mythical sea creatures, royal pageantry and bare-bottomed erotic encounters. The ancient imagination was laid out before our eyes.

We followed the raised visitors' platforms that ran through the chambers, Livia forging ahead while I paused again and again to let my eyes wander. Then, near the end, I stumbled into a small, rectangular room and saw them. The girls in bikinis from the poster Oriana had in her workout room. There were nine of them intact, in two rows, laid out in thousands of stone shards. They were far bigger than I'd thought—human height. The two girls in Oriana's poster, one lifting weights and the other throwing a discus, stood at the upper-left corner. The others were in mid-run or playing what looked like volleyball or some game with a wheel on a stick. One—the winner of the games, I assumed—wore a crown of roses and held a feathery palm leaf. Each girl was formally linked to the next through an outreached arm or the direction of a gaze focused on a ball in mid-air. This wasn't the ancient equivalent of a magazine spread; there were no pouts and poses. These were young women whose bodies radiated pleasure, who, like the women in my aerobics class, might enjoy being admired, but whose satisfaction came from an innate sense of self worth.

As I stood there I felt a tug of grief. I'd worked so hard and been so conscientious. In fact, I'd approached each day as if it were a moral obligation. And because of that I'd missed out on something elusive but key. Something these frolicking girls from almost two thousand years ago hadn't. I wasn't sure what it was, but it had to do with pleasure, with giving it its due.

Livia was waiting for me outside on a bench in the shade, batting the hot air with the Chinese paper fan she carried everywhere. I leaned my head on her shoulder and cried a little. She put her arm around me but it was too sticky for both of us, so she fanned us instead. After a while I sat up. "Am I boring?"

She looked at me. "Boring? No, I wouldn't say boring. Maybe too proper."

"Proper? There's nothing proper about me."

"You are very proper," she said. "But it's OK. You're funny too. I don't know. I just like you."

When I got back from vacation I was summoned for a meeting with the ambassador. From his expression I thought he was going to lecture me some more about the staff having too much fun. Instead he began talking about the Balkans, how the mission there had been plagued with problems, how they needed someone reliable to impose some order. He'd recommended me. If I accepted, my options for "interesting postings farther down the line" would be greater. This was foreign affairs speak for "there's no saying no." I'd be leaving for Pristina in a month.

At my last workout class the women looked as exquisite as ever. Giorgina seemed even more fit, if that was possible, and wore a new camel-and-cream-colored outfit. I couldn't be sure, but Patrizia's eyes looked wider apart and I suspected she'd been to the plastic surgeon. Oriana greeted me warmly, kissing both cheeks. She was golden-skinned and seraphic, but I also detected a hairpin line of stress in her composure. I wondered if the investigation into Cesare's business dealings would undo some of her poise or if the scandal would be just another thing to drop wry comments and shrug about during aerobics. I suspected the latter, and I was sorry I wasn't going to be around for the performance.

I didn't plan on telling Oriana or the others that I was leaving; I wanted to avoid awkward goodbyes. I hadn't penetrated their lives and I thought their final *ciaos* would have been strained. But at the end of my last class I told them anyway. They cried out *"Mi dispiace!"* and gave me their full attention for a few minutes while I told them about my new posting. I sensed some relief, but it didn't matter. They'd given me a glimpse into their world of astonishing privilege and, coming from them, that in itself was an act of generosity.

As I was leaving, Giorgina invited me for a final coffee in the nearby piazza. We sat down just as the sun cast a blazing pink streak across the sky.

"I wanted you to know that everything is finished," she told me. "Colleen-a, I am so relieved I was capable of doing it."

"You left your husband?"

"Oh, *per carità*, no!" she exclaimed. "With Pierangelo, we are very good. I am the luckiest woman in the world."

"Well, that's good." I tried to hide my surprise at the quick turnaround. "Is he spending more time at home now?"

"No, that is the same as before. Work, work, work. But I am not at home now, too. I have opened a store. *Alta moda*. Come by and I'll give you a nice discount."

As if. But I thanked her anyway.

"I'm curious," I asked. "What happened with the other man? The man in the park?"

"Oh, *that*," she said, waving her hand dismissively, as if Gianluca had been nothing but a minor irritation. "I discovered I was not capable of betraying Pierangelo. Simply not *physically* capable, you understand?"

Giorgina caught my grin. "Please, Colleen-a," she said, giving a haughty sniff. "A few kisses in the park. That can happen to anyone. Even the most happily married woman can find herself kissing someone in the park. Don't be naive."

She flicked a strand of hair off her shoulder.

"Anyway," she went on, "one day I phoned Pierangelo at work and I said, 'You must come home immediately because I have something I must tell you.' And he came. Right away. He understood, no?" She laughed. "Or maybe he was scared I was leaving!

"I told him everything. I said, 'Pierangelo, I need help. I have been swept off my feet and I am terrified something will happen with this man. And that it will destroy us.'"

"So you *did* talk," I pointed out, glibly.

"Well, a little, yes. Pierangelo insisted to know the name of this man and I refused, of course. But he is not stupid. He understood immediately who it was. He regarded me and he said, 'Giorgina, I thank you for telling me. I will take care of this situation.'"

Mafia clichés sprang to mind: Gianluca receiving a phone call and then hastily packing a suitcase, never to be heard from again. Or dissolving in a vat of acid. I tried to cajole Giorgina into telling me more, but she wouldn't. She merely smiled like the cat who'd got the cream and said, "*E' un grand'uomo, Pierangelo*. He's a great man, my husband. A *real* man."

Whatever Pierangelo had done, after years of marriage he'd made Giorgina feel wanted again, made her fall back in love with him. And having the will and the imagination and the gumption to do that was something I could only admire.

The Sunday before I left for Pristina, Livia came over to say goodbye. She was in her bakery garb, her hair dusty with flour; yet she still managed to shimmer, as if all the Mediterranean sun she'd absorbed on the beach was lifting off her skin and warming the air around her. She looked fragile too, and I was aware for the first time how much courage and effort it took to shine like that.

"Here," she said, thrusting a silver gift bag into my hand. Fuchsia tissue paper flamed out the top.

I stuck my hand in and pulled out a slippery rope. The strap of a gold lamé bikini top.

Livia said, "And now we go. Your last day at the Italian beach."

And we did. We lay under the gentle Italian October sun, Livia in her leopard-print bikini and me beside her, my breasts and crotch shimmering like three golden beacons.

I hadn't lost a pound. Despite all the sweating at aerobics, the food had proven too tempting. I'd be lying if I said I regretted it. And if I were totally honest I'd have to admit the food did take the edge off the loneliness that I'd been carrying around long before Rome, long before Gwen. A pang that might be part of who I was.

But I'd made a friend. And I'd ridden through Rome on the back of a Ducati. And at the age of forty-three I was wearing my first bikini.

I stretched and breathed in the warm, salty air.

That was all right. That was enough.

Motion

THEY HEADED NORTH IN THE MINIVAN, bikes on top and strapped to the back. When they reached Milan it began to rain. It rained the whole rest of the drive up, the water smashing down on the roof in angry fits as if to say, *Blue skies and good times? Take this!*

The Deweys sat in the front and took turns driving—it was their vehicle—keeping up a cheerful prattle about their honeymoon bike trip along the Danube fifteen years earlier. "The Wiener schnitzel were the size of pizzas," Denis said, twisting around to look at Claire and Frank in the middle seats. He formed a circle with his hands. "Each night we had one of these mega-schnitzels, plus a pint of that beer. What did they call that beer they have there, Lillian?" He turned to Lillian, who was arched forward and frowning in concentration as she drove. "*Weisse. Weisse bier,*" she said. "From wheat."

"*Jawohl! Das* is right. *Weisse,*" Denis said, stretching out the German S's. "And at the end of every meal—Black Forest cake. All that beer and meat and cream and cholesterol and we didn't gain a pound the whole trip. Came out exactly even!" He chuckled. "That's the beauty of a cycling trip."

The Deweys' son, Jason, was in the back seat of the van with Nico, playing some guessing game involving licence plate numbers.

The boys went to the same school in Rome, where Denis and Lillian had approached Frank and Claire at a kids' art show. Denis was about fifty, with thinning sandy hair and a boxed-in energy that made Claire think of a bulldog. He said, "I was just saying to my wife that you two look like the only ones in the bunch fit enough to handle a vacation away from the beach."

He raised his chin in the direction of the buffet table, where a crowd of fathers were jabbing at mozzarella balls and prosciutto, as if to say, "Italians! What can you do?"

Then he turned to Lillian and said, "My wife was a swimmer and I used to row. Competitively, too. Our one condition for a holiday is being on the move."

Lillian's lips pinched in at the corners and lifted into a tight smile. She looked about ten years younger than Denis, tall with curly black hair that fell to just above her swimmer's shoulders. She wore round glasses and had downward sloping eyes with heavy lids and an intense gaze. Later Denis told them that she was a tax auditor, a Bostonian, like him. Denis had been her advisor at college. Now she headed up a forensic auditing team for the UN in Rome. "I'm just along for the ride," Denis chuckled, then pulled a serious face and winked as if what he said next was to be kept strictly between them. "I'm actually working on a project of my own."

Even before she knew that Lillian was a forensic auditor, Claire thought she had the look of someone who found what she set out to find. When Lillian finally spoke she leaned in close to Claire and squeezed her elbow for emphasis. "When Jason said he wanted to go on a bike trip, I said, 'All right. Then it's the whole nine yards. A full day every day. No half measures.'"

Claire had recently read a magazine article on happiness. A study had found that everyone has an inborn predisposition toward happiness or unhappiness. You were born, say, fifty percent happy, or if you were lucky, eighty percent. But beyond this genetic inclination, leading a happy life was a matter of planning and making the right choices—choosing the right spouse or career or place to live. Deciding what would render your life smoothest or most fulfilling or most pleasurable and following through. Of leaving as little as possible to chance. The Deweys struck Claire as a couple that'd be able to spot happiness at a distance, go after it and wrestle it to the ground. Put a leash on happiness, harness it. And despite her ambivalence toward them—the little prickle they set off in her, like an internal rash—she allowed Frank to decide the matter of the vacation. He said yes. Yes, a bike trip together sounded great. Let's get together and plan.

On the way home from the art show, Claire asked Nico, "So, do you like this kid? What's his name, Denis and Lillian's son?"

"Jason," said Frank.

"Yeah, I like Jason," Nico answered. "He's got this cool model of the Coliseum with gladiators. His dad made it. And his mom was in the Olympics."

"You don't have to come if you don't want to," Frank said to Claire.

"No way, Mom," said Nico. "It's decided. You're coming with us or else."

She could have spoken up. She could have said to Denis and Lillian that she'd like to think about it or that, no, a bike trip really didn't appeal to her. All that fresh air and exercise. She could have said that after so many years in Rome she'd become too Italian. That she'd actually rather lie on a beach or sit under some awning in the countryside and drink decent coffee, smoke the odd cigarette and read. It wouldn't have been out of character for her to offer up some apparent weakness with a shrug, as a way out. As Frank pointed out, half admiring, half exasperated, Claire did exactly what she felt like most of the time.

It was true: Claire did, more or less, just what she wanted. They'd moved to Rome because of her, because she had fallen in love with the city. And they'd been lucky; she'd found steady work as a translator and teaching photography. Frank managed to get an import-export business going, so they were able to stay. Claire spent weekends at art exhibits or working on her photographs. With the exception of a few close friends, she preferred being on her own. Frank was the one who needed people, to get from them, Claire suspected, some reassurance about himself that she couldn't supply. Or that some stubborn part of herself refused to.

And as for Nico, while it would have been a stretch to say that Frank did most of the parenting, it would have been just as much of a stretch to say that she did. Nico was as low-maintenance as nine-year-olds come: quiet, self-sufficient and naturally kind. A kid who'd learned to tie his shoelaces at three, who happily spent hours with his building kits. Apart from a nightly meal and a drive to his music lesson once a week, Nico needed very little input. So Claire was as free as it got for a working woman with a child. As her mother had once remarked with a grudging chuckle over the phone, long-distance, compared to most women Claire was as free as a bird.

They left the van in Villach, at the Austrian-Italian border, where the rain gave the pink and yellow gingerbread buildings a glossy, overdone sheen. They'd booked a cheap hotel on a hilltop outside town: pine furniture, bunk beds, brown indoor-outdoor carpet. A waitress with pale, puffy skin served them greasy chicken and fries with soggy coleslaw, the only vegetable on the menu. The humidity released years of cooking oil smells and cigarette smoke from the upholstery and carpeting.

After dinner, Nico and Jason entertained themselves by drawing action figures on the fogged-over windows. Denis and Frank stayed at the table, heads together, poring over a map. They murmured about how much distance they could cover in the rain the next day and where the best place to stop for lunch would be. Claire stood nearby at the front desk looking over brochures. The river they were to follow was called the Drau. The Drown, Claire thought. The Drawn-out. The Drag. Lillian, who was scanning the guidebook for rooms to rent or bed and breakfasts, said several times, "We'll be out there, rain or shine." And even, "If there's a will there's a way."

They set off at 9 a.m., gliding single file onto the wet asphalt that followed the river like a line drawn in shiny black marker. The Deweys had come prepared with waterproof jackets and covers for their panniers. Frank had run to the closest supermarket for garbage bags, which they poked holes through and pulled over them. For Nico, raised in Italy where even going barefoot constituted a forbidden thrill for kids, the garbage bag was an adventure. For Claire it was wearing a garbage bag.

They were soaked within half an hour, right through to their underwear. Rain streamed into their eyes, ran off their noses, crept down the back of their necks. Claire seemed to be the only one not having a grand old time. The others chased one another to sign posts, called out back and forth, sang even. *"Row, Row, Row Your Boat,"* in rounds. Lillian suggested they sing it in harmony and got Nico, who despite years of music lessons was tone-deaf, to carry the melody.

"Wonderful, Nico!" she heard Lillian cry. "Good job!"

Claire followed Nico, watching his pumping legs, the rope of water cast off his back tire. He dropped back and cycled beside her.

"Come on, Mom."

"That's all right. You don't have to wait for me."

"Come on," he repeated. "Ride faster. You're slowing everybody down."

That night, after wieners, sauerkraut and fries, the boys went and sat in the lobby to play chess. The two couples stayed around the table drinking coffee with liqueur and whipped cream.

"So, I've been meaning to ask you, Claire," said Denis. "How did you get into translating?"

He sat directly across from her, tapping a spoon against the palm of his hand.

"Oh, it was gradual," Claire said. "I took languages at university and then read a lot in the original. I got pretty fluent and eventually realized I could probably make a living translating."

"What kind of things do you translate?" asked Lillian.

"Corporate reports and things like that. Those are the money-makers. Textbooks. History books. Sometimes the odd novel or book of poetry."

"Really?" Lillian asked. "Any bestsellers?"

"No."

Denis frowned, a frown to convey a disquieting thought. "Now, I trust you won't be offended, but it's always puzzled me why anybody translates poetry. Or reads poetry in a foreign language, for that matter. It seems a pretty sure bet that the translation's going to fail. I mean, given the nature of poetry, you can't expect a word in another language to relay the same meaning. Or richness, if I may."

"All language has hidden meanings," Claire said. "It's the risk you take. Every text becomes something else in translation. Even innocuous words like ... " Claire looked around. "Like 'watch' or 'hand.' They have a whole different set of connotations in another language. You just do your best to keep true to the spirit or intent of the original. A poem, a textbook—it's the same challenge, really."

"Oh, come on," said Denis, moving his shoulders impatiently. "A history book tells a string of events, albeit from one perspective. But it doesn't hinge on one word or image like a poem. There's hardly the same risk of missing its 'spirit.'"

"It hinges on an idea, an outlook that's just as crucial to the work as a word or line is to a poem. Something that can be just as hard to pin down."

"Denis used to write poetry," Lillian said, with a wry grimace.

"Really?" said Frank.

"Oh yeah. He had a reputation on campus. For that and a few other things," she added. "He was a real Walt Whitman. Back when we first dated. In the Stone Age."

"What did you write about?" asked Claire.

"Oh, everything and nothing," said Denis, dismissively. "I was in search of some universal truth, I suppose. Thought poetry might be where I'd find it. Got over that." He laughed, a flood of red flushing his cheeks.

"You don't even read poetry anymore," said Lillian.

"Nope. It's history I'm interested in," Denis said. "Novels too, but it's got to be something that teaches me something. With solid research. Something set in ancient Rome or Egypt or with a scientific subplot."

He cleared his throat, hesitated. Then said, "As a matter of fact, I'm working on a—"

"Or where there's a lesson," Lillian interjected. "A moral. A book with a moral. So you don't feel like you've wasted your time."

"Yes, time," said Frank, his eyes flicking over Claire. "There's that."

"I'm not sure I see the connection between a moral and not wasting time," Claire said. "Besides, what's wrong with wasting time?"

"Oh-ho!" Denis waggled his eyebrows clownishly up and down. "An unapologetic time-waster in our midst! I feel like I'm back at a campus sit-in!"

Claire had trouble picturing Denis as a college student, let alone at a protest of any sort. She said to Lillian, "I just don't see why there has to be the educational component. Why can't a good story be enough?"

"Because," said Lillian, leaning forward and narrowing her eyes, *"life's too short."*

The next day it rained even harder. Thick blankets of water fell in relentless succession, causing the cyclists to bend over as if receiving punishment. Frank and Denis led the way side by side, heads down, moving in sync like grimly determined pack horses. Just before lunch a fallen branch got tangled up in Frank's front wheel and he crashed. Claire looked up just in time to see him fall in slow-motion, like a careening tree, one arm braced against the handlebars, the other jutting outward, his spine arching to the side, his shoulders tensing for the impact. In what felt like a stretching of seconds, Frank's vulnerability radiated from him. It was a strange, graceful fall that thrilled her.

Frank got hurt, although not much. The side of his calf was skinned, leaving a raw stripe of pink. But his wheel was bent and had to be replaced, and that meant stopping for the day. There was a village nearby with an inn, so it was decided that Lillian, Claire and the boys would cycle ahead to check in. Frank and Denis would follow, walking their bikes.

When Frank showed up in their room a couple hours later, Claire was reading, her head at the foot of her bed to avoid the low slant of the ceiling. Humidity clogged the air, making the room claustrophobic. Claire had squeezed out her and Nico's clothes and draped the wet T-shirts, shorts, socks and underwear over a pair of electric heaters. Even with her dry clothes on, her skin itched. Frank came in and sat on the other bed. He pulled up the side of his pant leg and prodded his scrape.

"How is it?" Claire asked.

"Should be OK."

"You know," she said, "there's no reason why we have to keep going. We could hop on the train and be in

Vienna tomorrow for lunch. Think of that. Sitting at a café eating Sachertorte."

"I want to keep going."

"Why? I mean, look at us," she laughed. "We're not exactly having fun."

"I need to keep going."

"*Why?* To please Lillian and Denis? Show off your great *carpe diem* attitude? I feel like I'm travelling with the von Trapps."

Frank didn't say anything for a while. He had a haunted, pulled-down look, like his facial muscles had given up fighting gravity. "I need to say something," he said. "To put something straight."

"To put what straight?"

"How I've felt about you."

"On this trip?"

"No. In general."

"Oh."

"I haven't always loved you," he said. "I want you to understand this." His head bobbed a little as he spoke, as if he were egging himself on, following a script he'd practiced but wasn't sure he could act out entirely.

"That there have been times when I've doubted I've loved you. Actually, when I've been quite sure I have not loved you. Times I've considered leaving. I mean, seriously considered."

"Oh," Claire said. "Is this one of those times?"

"No. At least I don't think so. But I know I'm not happy."

"Why are you telling me now?"

"Because something has to change. And after thinking about it and talking it over, I've come to the conclusion that the only way is to push things out into the open."

"Who ... who did you talk it over with?"

"Denis."

"*Denis?*" Claire let out a little nasal hum, a plaintive, reedy note that scarcely conveyed her outrage. "*Denis?* You've been talking to *Denis* about me?"

"You're not going to get me to apologize. You don't like him—them. I know that. But I do. I respect them both."

Claire was crying now. "Why? Why do you respect them?"

"Because they're *solid*. They're straightforward. And they've got a ... program."

"A *program*? What the fuck does that mean?"

"It means they've made up their minds about who they are. They're not apologizing for it or questioning it all the time or vacillating. It's their outlook."

"So I've got the wrong *outlook*? Is that it? I need a *program*?"

"No. I'm not saying that. Maybe program is the wrong word. It *is* the wrong word. I'm just saying, don't dismiss them."

"I haven't dismissed them. I'm on this trip, remember? Riding right along with all of you."

"I know you are. And I appreciate it."

Claire laughed and wiped the wet from her cheek. "Good old polite Frank. 'Oh, by the way, I haven't loved you but I do so appreciate you coming on this trip.'"

"Oh please."

"Oh please? Oh *please?*"

They sat silently, the only movement in the room the quick rise and fall of their chests.

"You know what I'm thinking?" Claire said. "You know what I'm really thinking? I'm wondering if this isn't just a way of alleviating guilt. Is that it? Some convoluted, backdoor way of coming clean? Of telling me you've fooled around a bit over the years?"

"No, that's not it. I've never. Never cheated on you."

"No? Well, since we're being so honest here, I should probably let you know that I have."

Frank stared at Claire, frozen. "Oh fuck."

Claire had been in a book club once. It had ceased being about books, really; the women brought food and wine and met on Sunday afternoons to get a break from their kids and husbands. One time they were supposed to be discussing a memoir about someone's Chinese grandmother. Only one of them had finished the book, so the conversation wandered towards their own lives, which they were just as happy to talk about. In a conscientious attempt to keep the discussion related to the book, someone suggested they talk about their own grandmothers and what they'd passed on to them.

One woman spoke about taking up gardening and how, despite her lack of time and the backaches she suffered, she planted beans, zucchini and tomatoes each year as a way to connect to her childhood, when she had helped her grandmother in the vegetable patch. Another woman talked about how her grandmother had been the first woman in their town to drive a car, how it had remained a source of female pride in her family. Joyce, a sharp-witted woman with twins, who worked punishingly long hours as a lawyer, said that each Christmas she made the horribly sweet marshmallow squares her grandmother used to make, which she'd devoured as a girl. Her Italian husband and kids hated them, but each Christmas Joyce baked them as a small act of domestic rebellion and a salute to her grandmother.

Claire had only known one of her grandmothers, a cold, elegant woman who'd taught piano. She'd shown Claire how to read music and arrange flowers, skills that had had some use. But when it was Claire's turn to talk, she said, "I've had an affair and an abortion as a tribute to my grandmothers."

To her surprise, the other women burst out laughing.

"Right," Joyce said. "All the things that went on behind the needlepoint that we hadn't a clue about."

But that's not what Claire had meant at all. What women had affairs back then? Only the very rich or reckless, and Claire's grandmothers had been neither. Her other grandmother had been widowed when the youngest of her five sons was a toddler. She took in foster children with problems to make ends meet. Claire's father was the middle child. He left home at sixteen. The rare times he talked about his childhood he would always conclude with a pained grin, "We were never sure who really belonged in the loony bin, Mum or those kids."

What Claire had meant was that her tribute to her grandmothers wasn't in continuing traditions, but in putting an end to them. Seizing experience. To Claire that meant not only doing things her grandmothers would never have dreamed of, because their lives were circumscribed by children and husbands and stifling expectations, but also doing them without the mealy-mouthed justification and apology that even her generation felt obliged to offer.

She really hardly ever thought about her grandmothers, but they surfaced in her mind at interesting moments. When one of Claire's students fell in love with her in her first year teaching at the art college, for instance, they somehow entered into her decision to have the affair. The first time she slept with her twenty-three-year-old lover, she imagined she felt a surge of the suppressed lust of generations of women flow through her—she pictured a flurry of bonnets, gloves, petticoats and frumpy undergarments flying off along with her bikini panties. As she lowered herself onto her young lover, she couldn't help but smirk at the sheer indecency of it.

The affair had made her crazy for a few months—sex-obsessed, late for every appointment, frazzled, nervous with Frank and short-tempered with Nico—until she realized she wasn't getting enough out of it to make it worth the hassle. She ended it and felt relieved. But she'd done it, had said yes after all the no-no-no's of past generations. And even if she'd had the affair simply because she was restless and selfish, she was glad she'd done it. And before that, when she'd discovered she was pregnant eight months after Nico was born, just as she was resuming teaching, the thought of her grandmothers had come into her half of the decision to end the pregnancy. Or at least how she'd framed it. Without all the excuses.

On the fourth or fifth day—looking back she can't remember which—the skies miraculously cleared. White cotton-candy clouds sprang out against an azure backdrop. The river entered a broad, green valley and the hills on either side no longer felt like stern enclosures, but lush and velvety wings. They cycled past little towns with Hansel and Gretel houses and orchards dotted with plump, ripe fruit. Lillian and Denis were full of oohs and ahs and deep, satisfied sighs. Frank echoed them with the odd appreciative comment.

With Claire he was all tightly muscled solicitude; politely passing her the salt and pepper at the breakfast table, thanking her for finishing off in the bathroom so he could get in for his shower, instructing Nico to help Mommy with the packing. She remembered a friend who'd been divorced for years saying late one night after they'd smoked a joint, "I can't think of any guy I know who's as undemanding as Frank." Claire thought she'd meant it as a compliment until she went on. "I don't know how you live with it. Mr. Anything Goes. It'd drive me around the bend. I mean, does he ever tell you what he *really* wants?"

She'd been right, Claire thought. He gave her no sharp edges to grab onto and grapple with. In his own convivial way Frank had been stonewalling her. What was less clear was how she felt about it.

On the last sunny day together they had a late afternoon snack of sandwiches and fruit, then decided to keep on cycling toward a village where the guidebook recommended a bed and breakfast. Nico was tired, and a few kilometres before the village he simply stopped, got off his bike and said he wasn't going any further.

"Let's have a break," Frank said, and they all stopped.

Fields of tall, feathery corn lined the bike path and cowbells rattled nearby. Nico and Jason threw themselves down on the side of the path. Then they noticed a fresh pile of cow dung nearby and began tossing rocks at it, watching it splatter.

"That's enough of that," said Lillian, taking a rock out of Jason's hand. "You'll get covered in poop."

The boys wandered across the road to where Frank was sitting, morosely eating an apple. Lillian announced she was going for a pee and disappeared around the curve of the path.

Claire picked up a rock and tossed it at a cow pat. It missed, clapping against a rock. She tried again.

Denis came and stood beside her. "Here," he said, picking up a rock. "Like this."

He wound his arm up and lobbed the rock underhand. He missed. He rolled back on his heels, tipped his chin up and chuckled.

"Great technique, Denis," said Claire.

"Oh, I'll show you yet," he said, and threw again.

This one landed at the edge of the pat, sending out a splatter of dung.

"Well, some progress at least," he said.

"Progress?" said Claire, as she picked up a rock and threw. "Right. Because God forbid you'd actually waste your time throwing rocks at shit."

"Touché" Denis chuckled, pointing a finger at her. "You got me!"

As Claire and Denis took turns, Claire was aware of two things: that Frank was watching from across the road and that she was doing something entirely new to her—flirting with a man she felt no attraction to. A hostile, vengeful flirting she'd seen other couples engage in to get back at one another, to prove their sexual currency outside the marriage, to alleviate boredom. She found it desperate and distasteful even now, when she couldn't stop.

Denis stood back and put his hands on his hips. "So what do we call this? The Dung Toss? The Shit Hit? Now, how would you translate *that*? Oooh, I think you and I could have some fun with this one."

Behind them Claire could hear muffled calls and laughter coming from the cornstalks. Then Lillian came into sight, stepping around the cow pats. There was something both determined and precarious in the way she moved, like an athlete in the last stretch. When she reached Claire and

Denis, she paused for a moment and Claire thought she could see some kind of understanding—or recognition—register in Lillian's eyes.

"Where are the boys?" she asked.

"In there playing, I guess." Claire pointed behind her.

"And Frank?"

Claire glanced around. "Frank's with them."

Lillian frowned. "I'm not sure that was such a great idea. The sun's gone down."

"Call them then," said Claire.

Lillian gave her a sharp look. Then she hollered the boys' and Frank's names. Denis called, walking up and down the path. No one answered.

"Why on earth would Frank do something like this?" said Lillian. The sun had dipped below the mountains, the light on the fields turning grey and granular.

Denis strode off down the road.

"Have you ever *been* in a cornfield at dusk?" asked Lillian. "You can't see a thing. Nothing."

"They'll come out," Claire said, nervousness creeping into her. "I mean, it's got a circumference. It's not a like a lake or a cliff. It's not as if they can fall off the edge."

"Really?" Lillian swung around to face her. "Thank you for pointing that out."

Then she turned back and called again, a panicky shrillness taking over her voice.

Denis came back, stone-faced. "It's gotta be a mile deep. This is a problem."

"Well, why don't we walk down a side of the field each and call out," said Claire. "They're bound to be closer to one side."

"Didn't I just say it was a mile deep?" said Denis.

"Well, what do you propose then?"

"That we have your husband's head examined."

"Denis, that's hardly helpful," said Lillian. She walked back to where Denis had come from and called out Jason's name. Claire set off in the other direction, down along the field. "Nico! Jason!"

They called and called, walking up and down the road, the light ebbing from the dusk sky. No one dared to suggest they go get help.

Then, half an hour or so later, Claire heard Lillian's sharp cry: "Jason!" She turned and saw a small, distant figure making its way down the road and Lillian rushing towards it. Claire followed.

"Oh, thank God. Thank *God*," Lillian said, pulling the boy into her arms.

"We were playing tag and then it got, like, totally dark and I couldn't see anything. It was totally scary," Jason said, clearly shaken.

"Tag?" Denis said, incredulous. "He had you two playing *tag*?"

"Yeah." Jason looked around. "Is Nico out?"

"No," said Denis.

It was almost night now, with only a tepid light blanching the road and the tops of the cornstalks. Claire unclipped her bike headlight, switched it on and walked toward the field.

"We don't need another person lost in there," Denis called to her. Then when Claire didn't stop, he turned to Lillian and said, "Well, I guess that means I'm going in with her … "

"*Absolutely not*," Lillian said.

Claire pushed through the stalks, the beam from

her bike light bouncing off the thick, wide leaves. She moved slowly, her feet sinking into the dry, cushiony soil. She concentrated on counting the stalks as she passed to keep oriented, grasping their rough skin and pulling herself forward. *Eighteen, nineteen, twenty.* At thirty, she turned right, the direction Jason had come out from, and began calling out for Frank and Nico, her voice thick and stunted. The light created wild patterns that twitched and jerked with her movements.

She walked faster and stopped counting, a peculiar exhilaration growing in her. She felt at once enveloped and completely, utterly unencumbered. Alone and free and lost. She was overcome with an urge to shed her clothes and race down the aisles of corn, hooting and cackling like some farm wife gone off the deep end.

And then her light picked up something red. Then the flash of metal. The egg-white glow of eyes. Frank's. She held the light steady on him. Frank, lit up, as overexposed as a ghost, with Nico behind him.

"It's me," she cried. "Over here!"

"Mom!" Nico yelped and pushed through the stalks toward her light, grabbing her arm at last and wrapping himself around it. "We can't find Jason."

"He's out," she said. "Come on. Let's just walk in one direction."

When they approached the edge of the field, Claire felt a hard hand on her shoulder. "You let someone else in," Frank said, "and I didn't know. And *I'm mad.*"

Claire always thinks of the day at the lake as coming after the cornfield. She thinks of it as the closing act of the trip with the Deweys, a kind of denouement, although it wasn't. The end with the Deweys came the morning after the cornfield incident. Frank, who never got sick, woke up with a raging fever that kept him in bed for three days. The Deweys left early that morning to continue on to Vienna, and they did not see them after that.

But on one of the earlier, sunny days before the end of the trip, they'd stopped at a little bar on a dock that had paddleboats and canoes for rent. The boys went with an adult each: Nico with Frank, Jason with Lillian. That left Claire with Denis.

They pedalled away from the others, out towards the middle of the lake. Claire steered, pushing hard with her legs as if pedalling was the only way she knew to express herself, as if everything she could and could not communicate was channelled into those moving legs, up and down and up and down, trapped in motion.

Then, suddenly, Denis dug in his heel and blocked the pedals. He sighed—an indulgent, gosh-this-is-beautiful kind of sigh—and nodded at the mountains surrounding the lake, as if by merely existing he had helped the magic of the landscape come into being. Claire felt astonished that people this far along in life could still believe that their extravagant good fortune was somehow of their own making.

Denis reached out toward the boat's rudder handle to change direction, but Claire's hand remained on it. He kept his on hers, though. Did not move it. She wondered if he expected her to move and what he would do when he realized she would not. But he just kept his hand on hers, perfectly still. Nothing but light, steady pressure. Holding her there.

"An ode to Chiara," Denis announced.

Then in a low, intimate voice he began to recite a poem. Claire didn't recognize it, but as Denis went on she realized that it was his and that it was about her, Claire—*chiara*, clear or bright in Italian. She couldn't follow it, couldn't move her mind along the string of words that this man was attempting to capture her with. Only the last lines, which Denis delivered with affected irony, like the final line of a limerick, registered. " ... *Watch her true beguiling nature / not Chiara, but opaque / betray.*"

Denis didn't look at her when he finished, but lifted his hand off hers with a pat and waited.

Claire felt an immense wave of irritation and impatience. The poem was a deliberate intrusion, but she sensed that it was also a come-on. A sad, arrogant advance. That Denis wanted to provoke her—because even a negative reaction created a charge. A connection.

Claire pushed down hard with her legs on the pedals to get them churning again. (She would not tell Frank about this. Later, yes. But not now.) Without a word she steered them back to shore.

One night after Frank's fever had passed, he turned to her in bed and let out a heavy, surrendering groan. "*I'm in pain.*"

"I know," she said. "I am too."

He closed his eyes and stretched his arms out to her. Claire slid into them and was surprised by the fierceness of her desire. After they made love she cried—from both sadness and release. She wondered if the distance, their diverging experience and interpretation of their lives, was, in the end, a way of keeping things going, of creating fresh rifts that kept them struggling back to each other. And that while the struggle couldn't be called happiness, it had purpose and meaning that was no less valuable.

When she thinks back on that trip years later, the first picture that comes to her mind is of Nico. His little legs pumping, the white soles of his shoes flashing, his spine delicately curved as he charges ahead. What a fragile thing it seemed—seems—the force that propelled his small body forward in space and time, bravely and without a glance back.

She also sees herself. Always trailing behind. Trying to stretch out the space between herself and her family, herself *in* her family. To finally get perspective, to put things in focus. So she could decide.

Late in the afternoon on the last day of the trip, when it was just she and Frank and Nico, she fell so far behind them that when she came to a fork in the road, they were gone. She listened for their voices or her name being called, but she could hear only the dense, screeching chorus of the cicadas.

She remembers it dawning on her then as she straddled her bike (though more likely it had been a slow, unfolding awareness that took years), that her life was not determined by choices at forks in the road. That no matter which way she turned, she would find herself pedalling along with pain and tenderness and doubt. Always the doubt. Despite her effort to steer clear of the push-towards and pull-away, it kept blowing at her like a sweet, hungry wind. Less powerful over the years; with time, more like a wistful sigh.

But that day, when her eyes finally fell on it, on Frank's arrow made of dried corn stalks pointing right, she felt a startling surge of gratitude for being linked this way to another human being, and she followed it.

Let the Games Begin

IF YOU'D ASKED ME IN HIGH SCHOOL the odds of connecting with Guido Guancia, I'd have said about a gazillion to one. Guido was flabby and walked like a duck. These were traits I could have overlooked, but he was a glib know-it-all, which drove me nuts, especially when I faced off against him in debating. I couldn't dismiss him as a joke in that cruel, high school way— he was too smart and smart-assed to be reduced to that—but he was definitely not in my mind when I lay in bed with a few fingers between my legs, constructing a plausible fantasy that would involve me getting laid.

The funny thing is, I probably did consider the possibility of sex with Guido Guancia in my last year of high school. I used to play a game called Gun to Your Head with my two closest friends back then, Nadine and Mei-Lin, during our most forgettable classes. It went like this: If there was a gun to your head and you had to fuck five guys in the class, who would they be? I should point out that we were in the enriched program. This meant that most of our classmates were either brighter than average or totally average but desperate authority pleasers. It also meant that most were not particularly cool in high school terms. Pickings were slim.

Nadine's choices always included the teacher—she had a thing for older men—and the odd time, if the class was particularly unpromising, she'd put a girl on her list. She even put me there once, which kind of freaked me out, but at the time she'd been reading a book that portrayed intercourse with men as gross and unnatural, and I think she was pressuring herself to become a lesbian. Mei-Lin made her selections based strictly on who would be the least repulsive with no clothes on. Her list never included teachers. Mei-Lin pulled off the highest marks, but she was astonishingly superficial. She actually skipped school one afternoon to go to the hairdresser after Nadine noticed her cut was slightly lopsided. Anyway, Mei-Lin went for late bloomers, the guys who in Grade 9 looked exactly like they had in Grade 7 and 8 but showed up one September, usually in Grade 11 or 12, six feet tall with a brand new baritone voice and suddenly looked pretty good compared to the early bloomers whom you'd finally seen through after years of infatuation or who were working on beer bellies or serious drug problems from all the in-group partying.

Nadine and Mei-Lin hated my taste. They invariably reacted to my picks with an eye-rolling groan. Where I saw shy and sensitive, they saw self-absorbed and neurotic. None were what you could classify as friendly; Mei-Lin coined them the "Frosted Flakes." Objectively my picks *were* off the beaten path and if there really was a gun to my head, which was unlikely in Canada, my list might have been closer to Mei-Lin's or even Nadine's. But I didn't care if the guy was riddled with zits or had a terrible slouch. If he looked brooding and troubled, he piqued my interest. I couldn't help it. As for the fucking part, well, what did I know? It was just a game, after all.

Fantasies aside, I made it through high school a virgin—and not from a lack of options. I was tall and slim with a head of thick, curly, light brown hair, wide brown eyes and plushy lips that to this day are the envy of my friends, or so they say. My teeth are a little too small for my mouth, but these same friends tell me that's endearing. I look back at yearbook pictures, especially at my Grade 11 fencing team photo where you get a good look at my legs, and am bowled over: I suspected I was good-looking then, but I had no idea just how good.

A major clue, and in retrospect I should have relaxed and enjoyed it, was that I often got asked if I was the younger sister of Ms. Shit Hot, who was a year ahead of me. Janey Jefferson. My downtown school didn't have much of a sports field, let alone cheerleaders or a football team, but if it had, our Janey Jefferson would have been swinging her pom-poms and freezing her ass off, whooping her devotion to the center forward or quarterback or whatever. But since the school had a good music program, Janey sang in a jazz trio that vamped it in numbers like "Hey Big Spender" at the school's variety night. The guys ate it up.

Nobody exactly ate me up, or out, but they did flirt. Especially guys a few grades ahead. The interest in me might have been, at least in part, because of the Janey Jefferson association, although at the time I was oblivious to the possibility because, frankly, I felt superior to Janey. For one, I was smarter—that was easy enough to tell by checking out the honors list posted outside the principal's office. And second, I was a teenage aberration; at the developmental stage where the desire to belong usually dominates, I really didn't care what my cohorts thought of me. And Janey *really* did.

Smiles here, finger-waving there, tender hugs in the hallways with her confidantes and public, tongue-active necking with her boyfriend du jour. Janey was all casual sexiness: jeans with just a tease of a rip at the knee, sweaters a tad too wide at the shoulder, a hint of blush, but not enough to prove it. She even managed to get her mug on the front page of a national magazine when John Lennon died. She'd followed the hordes down to city hall like a modern-day Mary Magdalene. At the weepy vigil she was immortalized in the soft, flattering glow of her candle with tears trickling down her cheeks. It was the height of hypocrisy: Janey had been organizing a disco night in the school gym, which was hardly congruent with devotion to John Lennon. But Janey got away with shit like that. She was so indiscriminately friendly. She even liked me, despite my obvious disdain, and once pulled me eagerly into her homeroom class to suggest we dress up the same for Halloween—twin hippies or hookers—just to confuse people. I pretended this was a super-duper, swell idea. How do you say no to all that enthusiasm? On Halloween, though, I faked being sick and stayed home, which was a drag because Nadine and I had planned to dress up as a used tampon and pad (ketchup) before Janey had approached me.

Getting back to me, the boys flirted and I did my best not to alarm or alienate them. But the second there was a whiff of moving beyond exchanging pheromones in the hallway, I backed off. Long conversations at a bus stop, hand-holding, necking and the rest I found slightly demeaning, but mainly embarrassing. I was a late bloomer—I didn't get my period until I was almost fifteen and hardly developed breasts at all. Hormonally, things just didn't kick in until I was almost through the whole high school ordeal; and when they did, physically mature boy-men scared the shit out of me. Even the late bloomers with their freshly dipped voices and twitchy horniness were daunting. While I wasn't sexually retarded enough to yearn for the prepubes, I liked safe and shy. Frosted Flakes. Yet as Mei-Lin and Nadine presciently pointed out, there's *safe* safe and *too safe* safe.

If only I'd listened.

I'll kill the suspense. I went off to university, got a master's degree in poli-sci, became a policy advisor at the Ministry of Labor and married a gay man.

I made this matrimonial selection in the early 1990s in Toronto, one of the most gay-positive, everything-under-the-sun-positive places on earth. Stuart had suspected he was gay, but was so relieved when he met a woman (me!) whose company and conversation he enjoyed that he was able to oblige me with a periodic erection and a commitment to lifetime partnership. If he often seemed distant or distracted, he made up for it by being so easy to have around. I thought, "Stuart's witty, Stuart is incredibly gentle in bed, Stuart is the most open-minded guy I've ever known." How many husbands happily spend Saturday afternoon making personalized greeting cards? It didn't cross my mind that he might be gay, even when he occasionally fell asleep while locked in intercourse. I mean, it was the nineties! Who would put themselves through the hell of repressed homosexuality when the dykes and fags seemed to be the only ones who knew how to have a good time?

My reasoning was evidently too sophisticated for my own good. After Stuart made his poignant confession— "You're the last person I ever wanted to hurt, but I'm passionately in love!"—we got divorced. (He had met Ricky while walking our dog, coincidentally also named Ricky.) When I told her Stuart was leaving me for a man, my mom, bless her heart, said only, "Yes, Dad and I knew he was gay. Everybody knew."

So … there I was. Single.

At thirty-five.

Let the games begin!

The first thing I did was move into a new no-pets condo. Stuart could keep his Rickys. Then I signed up to an Internet dating service, featuring strangers sorted by age, proximity and the class they demonstrated in not mentioning an obsession with oral sex or bondage in their introductory statements.

I began to spend a lot of free time in front of my computer. I'd come home from work, make myself a big frothy fruit milkshake with a dash of vodka to help loosen inhibitions, park myself in front of my laptop and cruise the dating site. I had dial-up in those days, and friends trying to phone me could never get through. My friend Penny, a psychologist and no stranger to the emotionally marred, urged me to get in touch with my rage toward Stuart, who she thought got off very lightly for having tied up my prime reproductive years while he assembled the courage to admit he was a fraud. But, frankly, I was glad to have Stuart out of my life and I had been ambivalent about kids anyway. Eight months after we separated, Stuart, Ricky the dog and Ricky the non-dog moved out to Vancouver to take over a catering business. Goodbye and good luck! I now wanted male acknowledgement and I wanted it swift and to the point.

There are many, many men online, many of them willing to provide sex with few questions asked. I took advantage of this willingness on several occasions. But cyber-searching began to feel like an addiction, and I began to resemble a grown-up female version of a ten-year-old Nintendo-holic, desperately playing the keyboard as I rode an emotional roller coaster of hits and misses. And most of my hits—men who made it past my rigorous, three-point screening process—were only hits in the technical sense.

Don't worry, this isn't one of those pathetic "listen to all the losers I've dated" whines that my still-married friends so enjoy. I will say this, however: I stopped spending my nights in front of the computer making contact with unfamiliar men after my third date with what I thought was a decent if dull film set designer. We were out dancing and started necking when the moment seemed ripe. Then he slid his hands down to cup my bum, slid his mouth to my ear and whispered, "You haven't got much in the way of tits, but you've got the best ass I've ever laid eyes on. I'd give anything to screw you there." Whoa! Bring on the sweet-nothing charm! He got one last rear view as I walked away. I vowed that was the end of Internet dating.

There was one guy, however, whom I'd committed to for a coffee. We'd exchanged a few brief emails and spoken once, to set up time and place. I'd decided to cancel, but Penny urged me to keep the date, using the old "falling off a horse" analogy—climb back up on the ol' saddle so you won't end the experience feeling bruised. The "round-up" was at 11 a.m. on Sunday morning at a café a safe distance from home. And who should be waiting for me but Guido Guancia.

He smiled gleefully, grandly flagging me over to his table, then stood up and laughed. It was his laugh—a hearty chuckle topped with a crowing presumptuousness—that set off the click of recognition. Until then he'd appeared to be just another slightly balding, thickening-around-the-waist fortyish white man, with a big nose and glasses.

"This is amazing. Great to see you after all these years," he said as he swept me into a jovial hug, like a long-lost buddy. Then he gave me the once-over and nodded approvingly. "You look good. Haven't aged too much." He sat back down and laughed again.

I was mortified.

"Have a seat," he motioned.

I was unable to muster even the shadow of a polite smile. "Guido," I finally managed, "I can't stay. I didn't want to stand you up, but something's come up."

"What?"

"A family emergency," I said, sounding completely full of shit. "I'm sorry to do this, but it's truly beyond my control."

I made to turn and felt a firm grip on my arm.

"Bull."

He was still smiling, but looked me straight in the eye with one eyebrow cocked. Then he sighed.

"Could you please just sit down and have a coffee with me? I promise I won't tell tales out of school, and if you still think I'm a conceited asshole at the end of it, you can congratulate yourself on how perceptive you were even as a teenager. Which you were, by the way. You probably even perceived the wild crush I had on you."

This was news. I sat down.

"Great," he continued. "And you can relax. I got over it."

This was vintage Guido. Raise the white flag, then the second your opponent lowers her pistol, shoot. He used the same tactic on the debating team. Well, the rules had changed.

"Fuck you," I said, as the waitress approached to take our order.

I smiled graciously and insisted Guido order first. When he ordered a second cappuccino, I asked for herbal tea and the Grand Slam breakfast. I wasn't the slightest bit hungry, but I wanted to underline just how different we were. Guido could sit and watch while I consumed every last pancake, over-easy egg and strip of bacon.

"No offence," he said as soon as the waitress left, "but you've lost some of your debating finesse."

"And you've lost some of your hair." It was a cheap shot, but just being in his presence sent me backsliding to teenage immaturity.

"Good one!" Then he cleared his throat. "So I guess I'll start the catching-up. I've recently moved back here and I'm totally out of it. I haven't a clue what happened to anyone after high school."

"You actually care?"

"Honestly? No," he said. "Couldn't care less. But I *am* glad to see you. Despite your hostility. Maybe because of it, I dunno. Guess I'm still a bit of a masochist. So, what's your story?"

"Forget it," I said. "You can talk if you want. I'll listen."

"Fair enough." Guido nodded. "After high school I went to U of T, then after that went to work for my dad's travel agency. I met my wife, Carmela, there. We got married. Then a chance came up to help my uncle in Rome with his business and we decided to move. You know, for a change of scene."

His coffee and my tea arrived. We spooned and stirred.

"Go on," I said. "Let's hear about the divorce. There is one, right?"

"Yeah. Carmela's from up north. Sudbury. She didn't like Rome. Didn't even like Toronto. Found them too chaotic. She missed her family and wanted to move back up north. I didn't."

"Kids?"

"Well, I can't. I'm sterile. Carmela didn't want to adopt."

"I'm sorry." Fuuuck! Get me out of here!

"She went back home at Easter for a visit, phoned a couple days later and said that was it. The marriage was over and she was staying put."

"Bummer."

"Yeah. You're the first person outside my family I've told."

I ignored this. My meal arrived. I sliced and ate.

"My family over there was good about it and tried to get me to stay, but I knew I didn't want to end up there long term. So I came back and found a management job here. I've connected with a few old friends, but you know what it's like. People are pretty busy with their own lives."

I spread and crunched.

"So now I'm dating people I meet through the Internet." Guido looked at me expectantly.

This wasn't going to be quid pro quo. "What are your interests?" I asked.

"Do you pour on the charm for all your dates?" He chuckled.

"This isn't a date. We're having breakfast."

"Right. You probably wouldn't consider watching hockey and baseball an interest, would you?"

116

"Nope."

"Well, I work a lot, so I don't have many hobbies, if that's what you mean. No needlepoint or stencilling my apartment walls on weekends."

He was joking, of course, but after Stuart he'd actually just scored a few points.

"But I've always liked games. I play bridge, poker occasionally. I used to be a Dungeons and Dragons fanatic, but I gave that up in Grade 12. It was cutting into my social life." Guido sipped his coffee and beamed his self-satisfied smile at me.

"So what are you looking for?" I asked. "A replacement wife or sex with a lot of different women or chit-chat over coffee?"

"Don't know. I guess in the long term 'a replacement wife,' as you put it. But, hey, if I get lots of sex before I reach my goal, that's OK too. Even just talking would be good. Carmela wasn't much of a talker. How about you?"

"I like games," I said, bypassing the question of intent. "I play chess, though never to the extent that it affects my social life."

"Great. Let's play then. How about next Saturday?"

I said I'd think about it, but what I really needed to think about was Guido Guancia. He disconcerted me. It was oddly relaxing to be in his company; I didn't have to worry about mincing my words. In fact, the less I minced, the more he seemed to relax. But I didn't trust him. What was he up to? I'm not paranoid enough to think that he was playing out some sick revenge fantasy harbored since high school; but I found it unnerving that he was so pleased to meet up with me again.

My competitive nature won out. My father had been a chess champion once upon a time, and when I was a girl he devoted many a Sunday afternoon to teaching me the moves. While I hardly played anymore, the prospect of beating Guido was too tempting to pass up. So twenty minutes past the appointed time on Saturday afternoon (keep 'em waiting), I showed up.

His place surprised me. I'd pictured him in an anonymous high rise of the kind separated men tend to end up in temporarily, but Guido lived on the second floor of a large Victorian house, neat, decorated in warm colors, with a modern, fully equipped kitchen that he navigated with ease. So many freshly single men seemed to believe domestic incompetence was cute. Guido didn't, or didn't care to appear cute.

He brought out a plate of bruschetta and we settled into facing chairs with the chessboard and the food on a small table between us.

"I've got to tell you," Guido said as he crunched on the toasted bread, "and I hope you don't take this the wrong way. But this is the closest I've come to realizing a teenage fantasy."

"What is?"

"This. You and me playing a game. Together. Alone."

"This isn't going to lead to you feeling me up."

"I know that," he said, unperturbed. "I don't mean that kind of fantasy. It just woulda been pretty thrilling for me to be in this situation back in high school."

"Would it hurt your feelings to learn that this wasn't one of my high school fantasies?"

"No. But if you'd beaten me, I bet you would have enjoyed it."

I smiled my first smile at Guido. "Right you are."

I made the first move.

Pawn to e4. Guido moved his rook pawn. This told me he didn't have a clue what he was doing. Let me just say I whipped his smug little ass in less than two minutes.

He asked for a rematch. The second time around it took me three minutes to run him off the board.

He suggested we switch to checkers for a more equitable game. I loathe checkers. I was forced to spend hours playing checkers with my grandmother each annual visit, and the woman never had the munificence to let me win. But chess with Guido was going nowhere, so checkers it was. We played. And played and played. Up and down the board. I took a bathroom break (very clean) and Guido brought out a tiramisu, which he'd made himself. We ate a bowl each and then went back to sliding our glorified plastic poker chips around. Whoopee.

My focus began to drift. Instead of noticing that Guido had two pieces closing in on one of mine, I noticed that he had long, articulate fingers that manoeuvered with grace. And that he had lucent brown eyes with little specks of hazel in them that were almost exactly the same shade of his sofa.

I made an inadvisable move.

"Yeeeessss!" he bellowed. "Yeeeessss! I won!" He jumped to his feet and pointed obnoxiously. "I won! I won! And more importantly ... you LOST!"

I wanted to slug him.

He sprang to his stereo, ferreted through his LPs and put on a record. ABBA, a group I abhor. "The Winner Takes It All."

Guido leapt around the living room, belting out the lyrics like some grand opera virago. He was unabashedly exhilarated—joyful triumph in motion—and fascinating to watch. I was amazed at how well he moved to the music and I begin to register his full physicality for the first time. Until then I'd perceived him essentially as an oversized head. Just as I was settling in for the show, he yanked me up and waltzed me around the living room. His body felt soft and hospitable and I gave in to the mood. We strode and revolved together. It was a warm and tentative first encounter. A trial and a question mark. A truce.

I liked, I decided, Guido Guancia.

That night I called Nadine in Boston, where she'd moved after high school. I hadn't been the only one foolish enough to marry according to my teenage taste in men. She'd ended up with her professor, who was thirty years her senior. She spent much of her non-working hours nursing him after his second stroke.

I hadn't talked to Nadine in a few months, but we plunged into the heart of the matter.

"Remember Guido Guancia? Debating, fat, duck-footed?"

"Yeah, of course. Let me guess: heart attack."

"No, he's still living." I paused for effect. "And dating me."

"Felicity!" she screamed. (Yes, that *is* my name, and there are no acceptable diminutives either.) "He was so obnoxious."

"He still is. But I've had to rethink what's important in a man and I've decided I can live with obnoxious. It beats repressed fag."

"Whoa," she said. "Guido Guancia. So what's he like as an adult?"

"Surprisingly OK. He still has a momentous ego, but

he was dumped by his wife and I think that proved to be a good humbling experience. He's funny. And it turns out he was crazy about me in high school."

She was quiet for a moment and then said, "You hated him back then. Especially when he beat you in debating."

"Yes, I did."

"I mean, you *really* hated him."

"Yes. I did."

"It makes you wonder about what they say."

"What do they say?" Nadine was always coming up with "they says" I'd never heard anyone say.

"You know, that hate's the other side of love."

This struck me as unworthy of response. "Well, I think I like him now."

"Have you slept with him yet?"

"God, no! I'm just getting to know him. I'm not even sure how attracted I am. It'll probably turn out to be one of those light, entertaining kind of friendships. You know, buddies."

Guido had asked me over for a rematch the next Saturday. When I got to his apartment we skipped the checkers and fucked like two virgins condemned to death. It was frantic, ecstatic, all-or-nothing sex. What Guido lacked in technique (talking hadn't been the only thing Carmela wasn't big on) he made up for in sheer tyro delight. We laughed and chattered and panted and tried every position under the sun. He was impressively flexible. We slept a couple of hours, then finished off last week's tiramisu and went back at it. When I came for the third time, he called out "hat trick!"—it was hockey season—and we rolled over, spent.

"I can't believe this," Guido kept saying. "I can't believe I'm lying naked in bed with Felicity Lowry. This is just unbelievable."

"Get a new word," I said.

"OK. Amazing. Awesome."

"Tell me more."

"Well, it's so strange," he explained. "You were just so *not* an option in high school. You held all the guys at a distance. You were ... what's the word ... "

"Confident?"

"No. More like ... arrogant. Yeah, arrogant."

"Arrogant?"

"Yeah. And it suited you."

"I was arrogant and it suited me? Like peach lipstick? Like a perm? What the fuck do you mean arrogance *suited* me?"

"It just did," Guido said. "It was part of who you were. Even if it was pretty obvious it came from insecurity. It worked."

"I wasn't insecure," I said. "*Au contraire.*"

"Gimme a break. All of us were insecure in high school. Some of us just came up with better ways of hiding it. You chose arrogance and," he said, rolling on top of me and sucking an earlobe into his mouth, "I can assure you it was very, very sexy."

I have sensitive ears. "That was an elegant last-minute save."

"Yeah. And 110 percent true."

Guido and I began to spend an awful lot of time together. While he was keen to present me to his family, I resisted; it was premature to run the gauntlet of his large Italian clan. But we thoroughly enjoyed each other's company and the games: I coached him in chess and he taught me bridge. Guido had terrible taste in movies, with a penchant for the sentimental, but redeemed himself on the music front with an exceptionally broad collection from all eras and genres. We spent hours listening to music, talking and having sex, usually in reverse order. Despite his staid sexual history, we quickly whipped up a very imaginative love life.

Simply put, Guido and I made up fantasies and played them out. Neither of us had ever done this before. I mean, he was a manager and I was a policy wonk; we bossed and advised, but rarely created. Probably because of our linked past, all our fantasies took place back in high school. I'm not going to list them in detail, God forbid, but suffice it to say that in our minds (and beds) we screwed a lot in school washroom cubicles, at center court, in the chemistry equipment closet and on the principal's desk when she was in staff meetings. Guido even got a blow job during a physics exam, although that was a stretch.

What charged these fantasies for Guido was the chance to "go all the way" with a girl of his dreams, which he didn't have a hope in hell of back then. What turned me on was the opportunity to re-script my high school sexuality without the pitfalls of a corresponding reality. I was the lustiest, cheekiest, most shamelessly alluring teenage girl imaginable. And each time we went at it, I got to be a virgin all over again. The fact that the high school Guido hadn't been the slightest bit desirable only heightened the excitement and the power imbalance. With me on top. Guido would do virtually anything to have me and, while he did have me each time to the enjoyment of us both, being desired so desperately was divine.

The sex was free and fun and strangely intense. I looked forward to it each evening and if Guido and I couldn't get together, I'd suffer withdrawal symptoms. For the first time in my life, I understood the agony of a cat in heat. I'd become erotically dependent at the age of thirty-five—and liked it.

All the time spent with Guido was eating into my friendships. Penny, who had seen me through some rough times, was openly annoyed. One night she insisted we go out for dinner, no excuses. So, over sushi I gave her the general gist of what I'd been up to with Guido. When I finished she gave me her fake-neutral therapist's look I'm always amazed her clients can't see through and said, "Do you and Guido ever do it without the games?"

I thought. "No, not really. No."

She sighed. "Why?"

"Why what?"

"Why all the games?"

I knew, of course, what Penny was getting at. That the games were a way of avoiding real intimacy, blah, blah, blah. But so what? These days, everyone and their dog were tenderly disclosing. Intimacy was everywhere. It was on TV, in magazines, clogging up the health section of bookstores. It was tinting the very air we breathed a turbid, misty rose. You couldn't take an elevator ride without hearing about someone's disturbing dream involving a horse and their mother or their latest antidepressant. It had become the currency of friendships and relationships and acquaintanceships—and it came cheap. You tell me yours; I'll tell you mine. Whatever happened to simply enjoying someone's company without all the secret-swapping? I didn't want poignant divulgence. I wanted to engage, to lock horns, to play. And for the first time in my adult life, I'd found someone game.

Guido and I began to take turns leading a fantasy—setting the scene and opening the dialogue. To lend more variety to the scenarios, Guido occasionally played a student teacher I had a crush on or the track coach, although his pot-belly made that one tough to go along with.

One night when it was Guido's turn, he built a scenario that had me in a short skirt and "forgetting" to wear my underwear to school. He was following me up the stairs to the principal's office, where we had both been sent for being late. Before we made it into the empty office (the principal had been called into an urgent staff meeting), I nipped the scene in the bud.

"We're getting repetitive," I said. "Can't you come up with something different?"

"Different? How different?"

"Different enough to surprise me."

"So you want sexy *and* surprising? How about I jump out at you from behind the cafeteria door wearing a sequined thong?"

"No, that's just goofy. Come on. Think of something original."

Guido thought.

"How about the roof?"

"No, it doesn't interest me. Too windy."

"A pool!"

"Too grungy. Plus I hate the smell of chlorine."

Guido thought some more.

"OK," he finally said. "I've got one."

"Great. Let's have it."

"But you have to promise to not take it too seriously."

"Is any of this serious?"

"All right. I'm standing at my locker. It's really late after school. There's no one around, and then you turn the corner and you're wearing tight jeans and a baggy, kind of off-the-shoulder sweatshirt."

He squinted at me and pursed his lips in concentration.

"And you come up to my locker and … you ask me if I have a cigarette … "

"I didn't smoke."

"Just pretend you did," Guido said. "So you come up and you kind of lean against the locker and ask me for a cigarette."

"I would never have done that."

"Well, here's the twist. This time it's not you. It's Janey Jefferson."

I laughed.

"So I'm standing there and I say … "

He wasn't joking.

"I say, 'I don't smoke, but I noticed a teacher left a pack in the staff room.' So you flash me that big, toothy Janey Jefferson smile, and then you say … "

He paused to think.

"And then I say … ?" My voice sounded tinny.

"You know, you two looked a lot alike," Guido explained, pleased at his insight. "In fact, this is actually pretty funny. On that breakfast date—the one you refused to admit was a date—I thought at first you *were* Janey. Now that would have been *really* unbelievable."

"Really? Why?"

"Why? Come on. I mean, *Janey Jefferson*."

"Yeah?"

"Well, it would have just been too much. She was like the … pinnacle. She was hot."

"She was an airhead."

"Maybe. But so what. Everyone can't be Ms. Einstein," Guido replied. "Besides, she wasn't really an airhead. She just wasn't academically inclined. But I'll tell you something: she was really sweet. Especially to guys like me, which most other good-looking girls weren't."

"Like me?"

"I wasn't even thinking about you. You were in a different category."

"Which category was that?"

"What does it matter?" he sighed. "I like you better now than back then anyway."

"I thought you had a crush on me."

"I had crushes on lots of girls. I *was* a guy."

"But who was your biggest crush?"

"I don't know. Look, this is all fantasy. I don't want to contaminate it with too much reality." He grinned. "I might never get another blow job during a math exam."

"Physics."

"Yeah, physics." He sighed. "OK, this was obviously a dumb idea. I was just trying to come up with something different for you." He went to take my hand, but I pulled it away.

"No really," I said. "Say there was a gun to your head and you had to choose me or Janey Jefferson, who would you have chosen?"

"A gun to my head?" Guido laughed. "Why would I need a gun to my head to choose?"

"Just say."

"This is idiotic. I've never even thought about it."

"Choose."

"No."

"Choose or the game's over."

"What game?"

"All the games."

Guido eyed me. "OK, with a gun to my head," he finally said, "I'd have to say Janey. Yeah. Janey Jefferson."

As the gun was imaginary, my options were limited. I got dressed and left.

A week went by and neither Guido nor I attempted to contact the other. I was a wreck. I'd been born confident, forthright and fairly immune to what others thought of me, and these qualities hadn't been ground out of me by alarmed parents. They got me through high school and helped me professionally. And now I'd let a man I met through the Internet (*Guido Guancia!!*) casually set off a land mine under me. I'd given him full access to Felicity Lowry in her prime and he'd chosen Janey Jefferson, *really sweet* Janey Jefferson.

I needed to talk to someone. I couldn't face Penny's unspoken "I told you so." Nadine would find the whole thing plain weird. My other married friends would get a vicarious kick out of my bizarre sex life and I'd already entertained them enough with cyber-dating stories. Finally, I broke down and called Stuart. Since I already associated him with humiliation, I had little to lose wallowing in more of it with him. We hadn't spoken in over a year. When he answered the phone I burst into tears and poured out my sad saga.

"Wow. You've really loosened up. We never got even close to doing stuff like that."

"Right. So I could pretend I was some *guy* from your past."

"Oh please! Let it go."

Gone!

"I feel … tricked," I said at last.

"Well, you *did* have fun … " he said. "Even if he did see you as a surrogate Jenny Jones."

"It's Janey Jefferson." Stuart had always been a crappy listener.

"Janet Jackson … Jesse James … " he said. "Let's call her JJ."

"Let's not call her anything. She's not the issue."

Stuart sighed. "So what is?"

"I was toyed with. And by a guy with shitty taste."

"Look," he sighed again, "I don't know Giuseppe, but … "

"It's Guido, for fuck's sake. Learn to listen."

"Guido, Giuseppe, whatever! Gatorade! Let me talk for a change," he said angrily. "I don't know this guy, but I do know you and frankly, it all smacks of paint ball."

"Paint ball? What are you talking about?"

For my birthday one year, Stuart had wanted to organize a party. Something different. I'd seen a billboard for one of those simulated war places and thought it might be fun. Stuart didn't. He hated anything that smacked of team sports and tried to talk me into one of those murder mystery evenings. The thought of spending an evening in a pale imitation of a tedious Agatha Christie narrative was more than I could bear. Paint ball won out.

About twenty friends gathered in a once-productive factory now carpeted in sand and strewn with burnt-out cars and airplane parts. We divided into teams and shot at each other for a few hours. But the good times came to a decisive end when Stuart nearly blasted off my kneecap with three paint projectiles. He claimed that without his glasses, which didn't fit under the mandatory goggles, he hadn't been sure if he'd gotten me the first two times. I could hardly walk for a month.

"You always acted as if I'd purposely tried to maim you," Stuart continued. "And that's so typical! You push people into doing stuff they don't want to do and then blame them if they fuck up."

"I hadn't a clue that paint bullets *hurt*. If I had, I never would have done it or pushed you into doing it."

"It was a *war* game, Felicity," he said. "What did you expect?"

"You were the *only one* who managed to injure someone. And that someone was your wife."

"In case you've forgotten, guns were never my thing."

"Unless they came attached to a man," I snapped.

Stuart shut up. I could almost hear his silent mantra: "Rise above it … Rise above it … " When he did speak, his voice was quiet.

"You know what I really think, Felicity? I think you like the idea of risk and you like the idea of being daring, but when the chips are down—"

I didn't hear what Stuart really thought. I hung up.

That night I pulled out my high school yearbooks. I flipped through the one from my graduating year until I found my homeroom class picture. Guido was in the back row with a full head of hair and his same broad, cocky grin. He and Greg Choy were giving each other bunny ears, their maturity level at the time captured forever. I was in the first row sitting cross-legged in jeans and a T-shirt, slightly apart from the group. I was smiling, my chin raised in a defiant and—yes, Guido had been right—arrogant smile. Looking just as I'd remembered feeling: a little above it all, a little apart. While I'd long been proud of the stance, all I felt now was the impulse to close the book for good and get on with the here and now.

A few weeks later, as I was heading out to the gym, the phone rang.

"It's me." I could hear jazz in the background. "Guido."

"Guido who?"

"I was a jerk."

"Oh, *that* Guido."

"And I'm sorry."

"Really."

"Look," he sighed. "I think I was feeling used."

"Really?"

"Yeah."

"By whom?"

"By you. Who else?"

"Wow. That's a first. I've never used a guy before."

"Well, I have felt used before," Guido said.

"How, may I ask, did I use you?"

"In some of the fantasies. I think I felt like it didn't matter if it was really me."

P for perceptive.

"Look," Guido said after a long silence. "I'll be straight. I want to be with you. But I have a couple of conditions. If you decide to be with me too, that is. And one of them is that I want to leave all the high school stuff behind."

"What else?"

"I don't want any more guns to my head."

"Oh."

"All right?"

"Let me think about it."

I thought.

"I have a condition too," I said.

"What?"

"That we have a checkers rematch."

That night, after I beat Guido at checkers, we made love straight up. It was both comforting and unnerving. I knew giving Guido a second chance wasn't my smartest move, but sometimes to improve your game, you have to expose a valuable piece.

As for the other games, we didn't discard them entirely. They were no longer our main course, but they did feature as an occasional side dish. Because it wasn't clear where we were headed in the medium term, we set our fantasies in the safe and distant future, in an old-age home. Widowed or as a couple of old marrieds, we'd play chess and bridge and poker to our hearts' content. Then, when no one was paying attention, we'd slip into the linen closet and fuck like death was just around the corner.

The Funeral

Iᴛ ᴡᴀs Aɴɢᴇʟᴀ, Nancy's colleague at the culture ministry, whose father died. Suddenly, at seventy-seven, of a heart attack. Five of them from the press office had been at the corner *caffè* having their mid-morning break. Amid the hissing of the milk steamer, the clap-clap-clap of cups and saucers and the shouts of the bartenders, they sat squeezed around a table listening to Giovanni telling them about his fruit arrangement.

"*Incredibile*," he said, pulling his chin back in disbelief. Giovanni was short and thick and his top-quality grey linen jacket strained under the arms. "*Non si fa.* You just don't do that. You don't eat the banana."

He had put out a fruit bowl at his birthday party the previous weekend, and early in the evening, Pia, a woman Angela had brought—one of her family's charity cases—had lifted the banana out, peeled it and eaten it. Right in front of him.

"*Incredibile,*" he repeated. He pinched three sugar packets together and tore off their tops in one neat swoosh. The sugar cascaded into the dark liquid. He stirred.

"I won't even get into the way she was dressed," he went on. "Excuse my secular frankness, Angela, but nobody gets that frumpy without the church's involvement. Those horrible brown loafers that only the female faithful would be caught dead in. And that blouse rising up to her chin like a crusader's breastplate."

"Oh, please!" said Angela, rolling her big brown eyes but not really offended. She was used to this from Giovanni. The two of them had been at the ministry the longest, Angela hired just before Giovanni, during a short-lived and aberrant drive to do away with nepotism. Unlike the newer employees, who had gotten their jobs when hiring returned to normal, she didn't harbor any niggling doubts about her merits. She wasted as much time as the others, but she also had her Catholic family, which seemed to put her on moral terra firma. "It's now the church's fault when someone doesn't dress to your taste?"

"Or dress like a whore," added Silvia. She had dark, angular features and the facial-expression equivalent of a no-bullshit sign. A few years back she had had a disappointing fling with Giovanni, which apparently gave her the right to say exactly what she wanted to him. "Which would be your preference."

Giovanni flashed a scampish smile. "I would never deny my appreciation for women who look like whores. Or who behave accordingly."

He slid a pack of cigarettes out of his jacket pocket, pulled one out, lit it and shrugged. He could spend hours saying one outlandish, offensive thing after another, all the while remaining not quite likeable, but something even better—the magnetic pole of the group. Always the rapscallion smile that let you know you shouldn't take any of what he said seriously. That everything, even his prejudice and cruelty, was a lark.

"I don't get it," Nancy said. "What was wrong with eating the banana?" Nancy had lived in Italy for almost three years, but still couldn't sidestep all the cultural booby traps. Should the woman have used a knife and fork? Had she sent out an unconscious sexual message? Was it apelike?

"God help us! And you work for the culture ministry?" Giovanni scoffed, pushing out a puff of smoke. "I mean, a few grapes or a strawberry, that's fine. But the *banana*?"

"It's the backbone of the arrangement," explained Mauro in his wafting, nasal voice. Mauro was Giovanni's shadow—a dark, flat stretched-out repetition of Giovanni whose loyal presence seemed to lend Giovanni substance. "It conveys a certain indiscretion. A lack of appreciation for the visual harmony of the display. It's like cutting the center out of a torte to get the marzipan flower."

"Or taking off all your clothes on a beach when you're old and immense, like the Germans do," added Giovanni.

Angela rolled her eyes and groaned. "Please, not the Germans again. Leave those poor people alone."

"Yes," echoed Silvia. "What do you have against the Germans? Did you get dumped by a German once?"

"Is it no longer politically correct to bash the Germans? Have we come to *that*?" Giovanni countered. "They come here by the thousands and go on about how corrupt and crime-ridden and environmentally defiled Italy is, while they flood our coastline with their obese, pale, lumpy bodies. Horrendous. It's aesthetic pollution! You can't go to a beach without some oversized, sunburnt Bavarian in your face. Why shouldn't *that* be considered a crime? The government wants to ban smoking in public? Fine, go ahead. Outlaw one of the few pleasures that don't involve regret. But please, ban public nakedness among those unfit to be naked, too!"

He manoeuvred his cigarette into his left hand and with his right lifted the espresso cup and drained its contents. Then, forming a neat fist, he covered his mouth and let out a natty burp. *"Pardon,"* he said in French.

Disturbed by the reminder that smoking might soon be banned, the others lit up.

Giovanni continued: "I can't stand Berlusconi! His candor about his facelift was in absolutely the worst taste. Tacky and undignified. And that ridiculous bandanna he wore after his hair transplant, like he'd just stepped off a pirate ship! Improve your looks, by all means, but for God's sake, use some discretion. Nonetheless, when he called that German politician a Nazi commandant, I kissed the very words on the newspaper. Go ahead, roll your eyes! But he's the only one since Mussolini with the balls to say what he thinks, who's not afraid to stand up to bullies like the Germans. Or the Communists."

"My God, you're a fossil!" Silvia cried. "Next thing you're going to say is how much you admired Pinochet."

"Within a certain historical context, he had a point."

Silvia threw her hands up.

"Was she German?" Nancy asked.

"Who?" asked Giovanni.

"This Pia woman."

"Oh, *her*. No, she was Calabrese, almost as bad."

Silvia shot out her arm to whack Giovanni across the head—her family had Calabrese roots—but Giovanni ducked and instead she caught Mauro's temple and sent his glasses flying.

"*Merda*!" Mauro whined, retrieving his glasses from the floor and inspecting them.

"You're lucky," he said, blowing across the lenses and sliding them back on. "These are the real thing, and I'll have you know they cost me an arm and a leg."

And then Angela's cellphone rang the "Macarena." She lifted it out of its teddy bear carrying-case and answered, "*Si*," and then said "*Si*" again in a voice quite unlike that of the group—a voice that registered the possibility of something consequential.

"*O Dio*," Angela said, her brown eyes wide and lost. "My father has died."

They all went to the funeral. Angela had assured them it wasn't necessary—it would be too much trouble, it was the thought that counted and, besides, it was too far out of town and would take forever to get to. But not to go would have been worse than eating the banana out of the fruit arrangement. Once you had committed to a group—and to all the coffee breaks and chatting and uncompromised time-wasting—you were as bound to it as to a mafia don. You showed up.

Nancy hadn't been able to get enough of all the togetherness when she'd first come to Italy. She'd come for love. Why else would anyone move here? Certainly not for work. Her relationship with Enzo had ended after six months, the day they were to sign an apartment lease, when he had announced that he felt *soffocato* and was moving to Ethiopia. (He got as far as a beach in Eritrea, where he lay for a month, and then moved back to his parents' apartment and reunited with his old girlfriend.) But by then his family connections had got Nancy the job as foreign press liaison at the ministry and she didn't feel like moving back to Canada, just another casualty of Latin love gone *poof!*

Never had she felt so embraced, so coddled, as in Rome. She loved the tiny daily gestures that shot out like spider's silk and wove people together. The way the women in the office looped their arms through hers as they strolled down the street. Or the way a friend would place a hand on her elbow or play with one of her rings when listening to some intimate story, with no awkward concerns about sending the wrong sexual message. She loved the way store owners and bartenders, once they got to know you, would let you run up a tab or would slash fifteen percent from the bill if you paid cash or wrote the cheque to their aunt, to whom they owed money. She loved the kisses hello and goodbye and the way that everyone in the office was polled for orders when someone went out for coffee or lunch. She even loved that, when someone was off sick, the others would enquire about them and appear really, truly interested in the full rundown— how she hadn't properly dried her hair before going out on a windy day, how her spine had begun to stiffen, how the sensation had spread to the rest of her body and a fever had taken hold and peaked and held at 39.8 degrees (always the *exact* temperature), how her bones had ached and her throat had flared up and, she swore to God, she'd never felt that *terribile* in her whole life. How she could hardly move and the only thing she could ingest was camomile tea with honey until her mother had finally appeared and made her some soup with real chicken broth, the kind she used to have as a little girl—you know, with little carrots and potato slices and just a sprinkle of real Parmesan cheese and a drop of olive oil—and how, slowly, after being almost sure she was going to die, she had begun to recover. Nancy loved that, even in late June, when it was sweltering in the office because God forbid anyone turn on the air conditioner and risk catching a cold, if someone asked to close the window because a *venticello*, a slight breeze, was straggling through the office and threatening to bring on the mysterious and nationally feared neck ache known as *la cervicale*, all the windows would be shut, with a grumble, to be sure, but shut. Now *that* was inclusiveness.

Yet she couldn't help but notice there was also a high-gloss flatness to their lives, to her life. Not quite boredom—it felt too polished and cultivated to be boredom—but if she tried to be honest, she might admit that nothing of real import ever transpired. All her colleagues had remained single or with the same person since high school, still lived at home or in parent-bought apartments in their same condominium complexes and had no plans to move out or move on.

They were the *privilegiati*, university-educated with contract-for-life government jobs. They'd been born too late for the student protests of '68 and were too comfortable to get worked up about anything. They had no student debt (universities were overcrowded and Byzantine, but free), no mortgages and no offspring. Their income was not huge, but every euro cent of it was disposable. They drove snappy imported cars and went to art exhibits in other European capitals on weekend getaways. They caught all the foreign films (dubbed in Italian, because who had the patience for subtitles anyway?). They made it to concerts by musicians from Chile, Romania and Mali, whose names they could roll off their tongues with the ease and precision of ordering a *caffè latte*, extra hot, no froth, with a sprinkle of cinnamon. They hired young eastern European or Ecuadorean women to do their weekly ironing. They found it perfectly reasonable to bother keeping up with fashion trends in optical wear and mobile phones. They wore sexy lingerie as their everyday undergarments and dined out so often that their expenditure on food alone betrayed just how little they thought of their futures. Save? Who saved? What for? Their thirties were sliding by, yet they were largely undisturbed that the narratives of their early mid-lives were unfolding like a lazy summer afternoon. If not for the darkening tobacco-stained grooves between their teeth and their face blotches from all the reckless tanning, they would seem to be in the full bloom of adolescence.

Nancy, too, had taken on these rhythms and traits. Occasionally though, more and more often, she was visited by panic, at first tiny, then acute, and recently so overwhelming that at times it paralyzed her. There was a slippery quality to her existence, an inability to wrest it from the sweet and unflagging triviality that at first had seemed the remedy for her North American nose-to-the-grindstone approach to life. On many an early morning she lay in bed, staring at the ceiling, heart racing, thinking how fast life was spinning by, how many bad decisions she'd made and how little she'd really done. She so hated to admit it, but she suspected she was in need of a good old-fashioned Protestant bottom line.

She fixated on her unpaid traffic tickets. They'd come, one by one, delivered by hand and mail: illegal parking, entering downtown on a weekday without the proper permit, electronically detected speeding, talking on her cellphone while driving, darting through a red light, making a U-turn in a (deserted, she'd thought) intersection, driving on a sidewalk to get around a car blocking her exit to the street. Nothing serious, nothing out of the ordinary. But there they all were, in a stack, waiting and ignored and enough to put her in debt for months.

The others all gave her the same, simple advice: *Non ti preoccupare.* Don't worry. They may catch up with you, eventually, perhaps. But it could take years, decades even. In the meantime, enjoy life. The government might issue a parking ticket amnesty, laws might change, records might get lost. There was always a way out.

And yet, Nancy did worry. She came from a place—a geographical, psychological, *moral* place—where a mounting pile of unpaid parking tickets was a major worry. It meant thumbing your nose at civil society, weaseling out of a just punishment. She suspected it revealed something soft and easily corruptible about her. If she could just deal with the tickets, with even the latest one, if she could only muster the guts to enter the bureaucratic purgatory of overdue fines— the serpentine line-ups, the ubiquitous misinformation about how and how much to pay, the relentless to-ing and fro-ing from Fascist-era buildings—she might get a grip on the rest of her life. She might put things in order. Not the order she left back home—she didn't want that—but a new order. But each time she thought of paying the fines or of finding a job that involved work or a man who could commit, she came to the tired conclusion (and this is when it crossed her mind that she'd been in Italy too long) that any one of these moves would be far too complicated.

They met in a large, trafficky piazza that featured a fountain of sculpted bumblebees. Silvia, Nancy and Pia, the woman from the party. The one who'd eaten the banana. She was pale and virtually shoulderless, with a bad dye-job, which the sun ignited an orangey red, leaving her roots a dejected brown.

Angela had called the night before and asked Nancy if she would give Pia a lift to the funeral: "She has to get to work right after, so don't worry about giving her a ride back."

The funeral was in Ostia, a down-at-the-heels second-rate seaside town squatting at the mouth of the Tiber. In ancient times it had been a bustling port, crucial to the Empire. Now, forty minutes from Rome on a good traffic day, it was merely a place where at the last minute or as a last resort, thousands of Romans spent a day in the sun. A place that, off season, was dead.

They entered Ostia and drove past large, vacant restaurants and up a residential avenue lined with beleaguered-looking apartment buildings constructed in the sixties or seventies.

"There's the church," Pia said, pointing out the window.

"How awful!" Silvia moaned.

It was awful. God awful. Bandshell-shaped with a jagged bronze crucified Christ stuck on the façade, looking like something an angry twelve-year-old had welded in shop class. It could have been any one of the suburban churches marooned in deserted parking lots across North America. Not a penny had been wasted, from the plain white interior inside the glass doors to the faux stained glass windows. (A penny saved is a penny earned, Nancy's mother would say.)

The three women stood waiting for Giovanni and Mauro on the sidewalk in front of the church, watching the mishmash of locals trickle in for the funeral. Pia seemed to know them all, nodding and raising her hand as they made their way into the church. The only ones well turned out were clusters of Somalis or Ethiopians, Nancy couldn't tell which, tall and ethereal, the men in crisp white shirts, the women in silk dresses. The Italians were mainly older, shabbily dressed, badly groomed. A woman with huge breasts swinging freely inside her housedress shuffled into the church in a pair of plastic slippers. Small-town, ordinary people you never saw in Rome, at least not in the Rome of the Spanish Steps and the Pantheon and cobblestone alleyways where a soft, distant sea breeze could rise out of nowhere and caress your skin, where the echo of footsteps sounded like the music of some exquisitely crafted wooden instrument or the ghostly call of a tropical bird. The Rome that in any light and on any street corner was so startlingly beautiful it could make you cry— had made Nancy cry the first time—for having settled for so much righteous drabness for so long.

It started off as expected. A white-haired priest led the congregation in prayer, the *Liturgia della Parola* that they tried to follow on the fuzzily photocopied handouts.

> *I confess to almighty God, and to you, my brothers,*
> *that I have sinned through my own fault: in my*
> *thoughts and in my words, in what I have done and in*
> *what I have failed to do …*

Nancy sat second to the end in a back pew, squeezed between Giovanni and Pia, who was next to the aisle. She could see Angela and her family at the front, heads bowed, hands joined in prayer, an anomaly bordering on the eccentric: devout, practising Catholics in a country where most people had dumped the content and kept the religious wrappings— mass once a year, superstitious heart-crossing, a Padre Pio picture hidden in their wallet. Monday mornings Angela would update them on the latest family drama from Ostia.

She spoke of her parents with mild exasperation. They went to mass regularly, donated an absurd portion of their income to charity, took in children and wastrels and, rarest of all, followed papal broadcasts to hear the pope's message rather than to speculate on how much longer he'd last. She depicted the rest of her family as a good-hearted but simple bunch. There was the hysterical older sister who'd chased away her perfectly decent husband and then had a nervous breakdown, leaving Angela's parents to raise her children. There was the dim-witted brother who lived with a former prostitute, another of the parents' rescue missions, whom everyone but the brother suspected still plied her trade. Then there was the host of adopted and foster children: the schizophrenic Guido; Mimmo, the one-legged gambling Sicilian whom Angela's parents had to bail out from time to time; and Valentino, with no legs at all, who was, of all things, a cobbler.

Nancy often wondered how Angela was able to knit the two parts of her life together: the tragicomic family with all its too-real burdens and the office crowd, people who got worked up over the centrality of a banana in a fruit bowl. Yet Angela seemed to manage effortlessly. It had something to do with her practicality, Nancy guessed, her refusal to give things too much thought. As if she'd made up her mind that there was nothing to be done about the circumstances of life, that circumstances, in fact, were all there were. As if Angela had decided to enjoy these circumstances as best she could, without uncomfortable introspection. To not pass judgement on anyone or anything. Nancy was in awe of this ability, but knew it was what made Angela so utterly different from her. So foreign.

The guilty pronouncements continued. Giovanni fanned himself expansively with the paper handout. Pia recited the prayers quietly, cheeks flushed, rocking back and forth with the words. Nancy began to feel queasy. She hadn't been at a church service since her early teens, when halfway through her confirmation classes, she quit. The classes were held in the church basement by a new minister, younger than the previous one, with dandruff and bad breath. One evening when her mother picked her up after class, Nancy announced that she would not be getting confirmed and she would not be going to church again. Would not "set foot in a church ever again" was how she put it for dramatic effect. Her parents phoned the minister the next day: What had happened to their daughter, who'd gone to church all her life without complaint, to make her decide in one night that she would never return?

Nothing had. Nothing more than the realization, as she sat in the church basement with its linoleum floors and fluorescent lights and the Dixie cups of grape juice, that she could not stand it. She couldn't stand looking at the minister or smelling his breath, couldn't stand sitting on hard wooden benches each Sunday, singing songs that were flat and droning, looking at the backs of men's heads with starched collars digging into their neck flesh. Could not stand any of it. Later, she put a word to it. She could not stand the *aesthetics* of churchgoing. But she also knew that where she came from, that was a reason that had no validity at all.

At last, the *per Cristo, con Cristo, e in Cristo* and on to the eulogy. A man in a wheelchair at the end of the front pew—it had to be Valentino—rolled over to a ramp at the side of the pulpit, pushed his way up and wheeled around to face the congregation. He had dark eyes with black lashes and eyebrows and a luxuriant mouth. He smiled, revealing brilliant, straight teeth. And then he began to speak, in a distinct, commanding, joyful voice that carried throughout the church. He spoke about his foster father. His devotion to his many children, adopted and fostered and his own, of the challenges and losses. One died of a drug overdose; another was still in prison. Valentino acknowledged the others, all of them with some personal challenge, some special gift. And the father who had loved them all.

Valentino paused, a long pause that made the mourners look up and shift uneasily. When his voice rang out through the church again, it was gruffer, thicker with emotion. Nancy listened closely for the first time. He began to speak of his father's career as an urban planner. Employed by the city for forty years. Always a supporter of unpopular causes. Here Valentino's voice cracked. One of the causes—his father's attempt, in the eighties, to secure immigrant housing—was especially unpopular. He'd launched a campaign to have abandoned buildings in Rome designated for this purpose. He'd stood alone in refusing the envelopes of money offered by developers to put up profitable condominiums instead. *He would not be compromised,* Valentino said. And he paid the price. The city managers couldn't fire him; they had no just cause. But they could give him no work. They could take his office away. They could isolate him. Eleven years without a desk of his own, without a real assignment! And never a word of complaint at home. Never a word about what he faced each morning as he left for work.

"*That* was our father," said Valentino. "*Uncompromised.*"

Nancy and the others swept from the church with the stream of mourners. The sunlight was blinding and she stumbled into the shade of the church wall and pulled on her sunglasses. The crowd seemed to have swallowed even more humanity and suffering during the funeral. People milled about, shook heads and held hands, wept and embraced.

"Oh, thank God, a bit of shade," Giovanni said, appearing at her side, dabbing the sweat from his forehead with a handkerchief. "I'm leaking enough liquid for a baptism."

Mauro stood beside him, wearing a pair of burnished sunglasses that curved and swelled around his eyes, making him look like an insect. "We've decided we're going to the beach," he said, "since we can claim the whole day at the ministry. Silvia's run off to get pizza and beer."

"Angela may join us later," Giovanni added, raising his eyebrows and casting a glance around the square. "If she can get away."

"I'm not feeling well," said Nancy. She wasn't. She felt dizzy and claustrophobic. She wondered if she was coming down with something. "The eulogy ... "

"Interminable," Giovanni said. "Went on forever. I was worried it would work up to a call for beatification."

"You didn't find it moving? What Angela's father went through? It was terrible what happened to him."

Giovanni wiggled out of his jacket and draped it over his arm.

"Yes, poor man, putting up with such treatment for so long. *Nil nisi bonum*, of course, but let's not be naïve. You can't go on like that, showing up like some saint, acting like you're the only one in the office who has principles. Of course you're going to alienate people."

"Alienate people?" Nancy said, feeling her heartbeat picking up, her pulse suddenly fluttering like a moth too close to a flame. "He refused to be corrupt. He bothered with people who didn't fit in."

"And good for him," Giovanni snapped. "They may well make him a saint. But those of us who aren't angling for sainthood—and believe me, most of the people he took in aren't either—we have to live in the real world. And whether you like it or not, my dear, that means getting your hands dirty." He wiggled his fingers in front of Nancy's face.

Mauro interrupted. "I'm melting. Can we get going, please?"

Giovanni looked to Nancy. "Coming?"

But Nancy did not want to get going. Not with them. Something had risen inside her stomach. An ugly, unexpected but fully formed feeling. Disgust.

Disgust for these people. Disgust for herself for sinking into this softness that seemed bottomless, for allowing herself to wallow in it.

Giovanni squinted at her. "Are you all right?"

"I'm sick."

He stepped back. "Ah, *si*?" Sick was an entirely different matter. Sick was serious. "Well then, you'd better not come. Get home instead."

She drove slowly, edging her way down the avenue in the small bottleneck created by the funeral. Groups of people passed her on foot along the broad, bleached sidewalks. Ahead, she recognized Pia hurrying along.

She rolled down the window and called her name.

Pia turned, surprised. She approached the car cautiously and stuck her head in the window. Two pink spots stained her cheeks.

"I'm going back to Rome," Nancy said. "Would you like a lift?"

"If it's not too much trouble. I was just going to the train station."

"No trouble at all."

Nancy felt that picking up Pia was the first decent thing she'd done in ages. She was glad to have Pia's pale, quiet presence beside her, talking in a hushed tone about the funeral and Angela's father and his dignity in the face of his trials.

Then Pia went silent for a moment, as if weighing what she would say next. "The same thing is happening to me, you know."

"What is?"

"What happened to Angela's father. The lawyer I work for, he's trying to get rid of me."

"Because of your politics?"

"Politics?" Pia said, as if the word left a bad taste in her mouth. "I have nothing to do with politics. It's because I'm older. Because I don't wear miniskirts and make-up like the younger secretaries do. He's actually said this to me. But the reason isn't the point. All that matters is that you won't change to suit them. So they try to get rid of you. Nobody says hello when you come in, they all leave for lunch without you. They lose the files you're working on. It's how they get rid of you here. By making you feel invisible."

"Can't you fight it?" said Nancy, though she knew how feeble it sounded. "Or find another job?"

Pia gave a small, bitter chuckle. "You know, I shouldn't even be a secretary. I'm a journalist—I have a degree. I spent twelve years working on contract, being paid nothing, really. Small change. And finally, when the job came up that I had been promised, they gave it to someone else. The son of the editor's friend. I couldn't get out of bed for six months after that. Because I knew that was it. With no connections, that was it. If it hadn't been for Angela's father, who understood, I don't think I would have lived.

"So you see," Pia said, with an imploring smile, "you see just how rotten this country is? All favors and cheating. You see what it does to people?"

Nancy did see. She saw what she had been trying to avoid seeing for a long time. That it was time to leave. Get out. Go home.

They sped past EUR, the sleek, oversized neighborhood built in the Mussolini days, along Via Cristoforo Colombo with its umbrella pines that ushered five lanes of traffic towards Rome. Ahead, a police car was parked on the shoulder and two officers were standing with radar devices pointed at oncoming traffic.

Nancy remembered her tickets.

She would have to pay them before she left. She *would* pay them before she left. Whatever it took. She would go and get in line—borrow money from her parents if necessary—and pay. She would get on it. Today. Deal with it and leave.

For the first time in months, she felt clear-headed. All her queasiness and anxiety were gone. She started talking to Pia, confessing really. She told her about the tickets, about the giddy sensation she'd felt when she began ignoring them and how comforting her colleagues' advice had been: Don't worry. *There's always a way out.* How obtuse she'd been.

When she finished Pia said, "So you haven't started the actual process of paying any of the tickets yet?"

"No."

"Then I can help you."

"You can?"

"Yes, the lawyer I work for. That's our main business."

"Tickets?"

"Getting people out of paying tickets. See, if you try

to pay them, it's complicated. And there are heavy, heavy penalties. It could take months. In your case, longer."

"Longer?"

"Yes, since you've left it so long. But don't worry," said Pia, with an urgent breathiness. "We've found a loophole in the law, you see: we get people off paying the ticket and the city pays instead. It even has to pay the lawyer's fee." It was as if a light had been switched on inside Pia, bright and purposeful.

"Sorry, I don't understand."

"There's nothing to understand. You don't pay. These new justices of the peace—they're not like the old judges who tried to squeeze everyone dry. These ones don't care who pays; they just want to push the case through. So we make up a story—it was impossible that you went through a red light or were speeding, because you were at work or visiting someone in the hospital—and then the ticket gets waived and the city pays our fees."

"But don't they know it's not true?"

"I told you, they don't care. They just want it done with."

Pia snapped open her purse and pulled out a card and a pen. All the hesitancy, all the gloom that had enshrouded her had evaporated. No fishing around for a card; no apologetic murmuring about being too forward. She scribbled something.

"Here, this is my direct number, but ask for me, just in case one of the other secretaries answers. And if I can't come to the phone, don't leave a message, the little shits never pass anything on."

She stuck the card on the dashboard.

"But I want to pay," said Nancy. "You see, I'm leaving. I'm going back home, for good, in the next few weeks. I've made up my mind. But I want to clear the tickets up. I don't want to get out of paying them, I want to pay and then leave."

"But you've left them too long. It's not a matter of paying the tickets anymore. You can't just go to the justice of the peace, hand him the money and that's that. It's a civil case now. If you decide to pay, you have to wait for the case to come through the courts, admit your guilt and then pay God knows how much. It could take years."

"Years?"

Pia bit her lip and nodded. "That's why I say leave it to us and we'll clear it all up."

"But—"

"Oh, pull over here!" Pia said, pointing to a side street up ahead. "My office is just around the corner."

Nancy pulled onto the curb at the traffic light. The light changed to green. A car manoeuvred around them and honked loudly.

Pia slid out and pushed the door shut. "Call me, and we can get it all worked out," she said through the open window. "Or better yet, come by and we'll go for a coffee. Or lunch." She smiled and winked and then backed away.

As Nancy eased into traffic again, she caught a last glimpse of Pia in the rearview mirror: small and drawn-in again, her mop of browny-red hair falling forward onto her face. But she also noticed something else: a sly determination in her walk, a resolve in her gait that kept her going, that was *needed* to keep you going.

The creamy, succulent smell of jasmine wafted in through the open window. The wisteria was out too, lazily draping its clumps of flowers over crumbling walls. Nancy steered towards the Tiber and veered right along the river, cruising under the sycamore trees whose mottled shade flickered over her like fingertip touches. She turned and emerged onto a grandiose bridge and into the limpid sunshine of midday. The wind shifted Pia's card on the dashboard, lifting it and dropping it in a teasing dance. Up and down. Up and down.

It was a gorgeous day. People were out in droves, lingering at outdoor *caffè* stands, promenading along the river. It was like the day she first drove through the city. She had experienced a kind of rapture, an acute wish to spend the rest of her life immersed in this. All of it. The boisterous tangle of street life; the warm, pliant strokes of a summer breeze; the sweet, sweet smell of Rome.

Saving Rome for
Someone Special

ONE FRIDAY EVENING in late May, just as Jonathan was wrapping up Caesar's stabbing on the sidewalk above the Curia Pompeii for a busload of high school students from Wisconsin, his cellphone rang. It was a barely audible Fiona.

"There's ... staying ... tonight," was all he caught between the line cutting out and the roar of passing Vespas and buses.

"I can't hear!"

" ... woman ... staying tonight ... Jeffers's friend ... awful happened ... need more wine."

Fiona's half-obliterated words still managed to deliver a potent double blow: first, the request for more wine could only mean that the superb Vino Nobile di Montepulciano he'd been saving had been drunk; second, the phrase "staying tonight."

"There's no guest, right?" he bellowed into the phone, and when a crackly silence ensued, "Right that there are no guests?"

"Stop yelling," said Fiona, in a sudden burst of clear reception. "Yes, there is a guest, but just for one night. The woman Jeffers emailed us about."

"What?"

"I didn't feel I could say no. She's had an awful thing happen. How would you feel about giving her our bedroom?"

"*What?*" They'd been idiot-hosts, granted, offering shelter to passing acquaintances of friends of friends or to anyone with a crimson maple leaf on their luggage, but nobody, not even Fiona's mother, got the bedroom.

"She's coming out of the bathroom. Don't forget the wine. Please."

As he surged through traffic on his Vespa, Jonathan tried to remember Fiona's brother's email. Something about a friend's ex coming through. Something about "it might be fun" for them to meet up.

Electronic missives headed Tiny Favor, Small Request, Question and Help! popped up like herpes in their inbox. Anything from queries about the weather and exchange rate ("Ever heard of Google?" he said aloud to these) to bulleted lists of questions about the pluses and minuses of travel itineraries, local festivals coinciding with visit dates, ways to get to and from the airport and how the Italian phone system worked ("Ever fucking heard of a guide book?").

They had been naive the first few months, they later said. (They'd been morons, he thought.) They'd sent out email chronicles of their big Italian adventure—regularly clicking "all." One month it was a bulletin from Tuscany full of hackneyed descriptions of crumbling ochre walls, the next, reflections on the soulful simplicity of fresh basil and tomatoes. They could be forgiven for those, Fiona said: noviciate enthusiasm. For Jonathan's wine notes, as well. (He once observed that a certain Tuscan red "closed with a definitive vanilla-anise-oak tang." Jeffers had replied that the only liquid tang he could relate to came in crystal form: add water and stir.)

But what really killed the updates was everyday Italian life. It soon overwhelmed them with its racket and guile and inexplicability. They found it impossible to differentiate between what was charming or noteworthy and what was plain freakish. Should they tell about the old lady at the *gelateria* who became so irate when they tried to pay for their ice cream cones with a twenty-euro bill (a *twenty*, Jonathan repeated, not even a fifty!) that she shooed them out of her shop and spat on the sidewalk after them? Or the small bomb that went off early one morning in the nearby Celtic bar, rumored to be a neo-Fascist hangout? Or the annual national holiday to celebrate Western civilization's ultimate non-event, the Immaculate Conception? Too much contextualization was required. They made "Pickpocketed in Saint Peter's" their last Note from Abroad. But not before Jonathan, in a burst of expat loneliness, sat down and invited "all" to visit. "We've got room!" he keyed, and sent.

They came. Like flies to shit, Jonathan observed. Alone, in pairs and in families of four. An endless succession of bodies on the pullout couch. And with them, suitcases and shopping bags choking the hallway; late-night chattering; peculiar odors loitering in the bathroom; constant editorials about just how crazy it was that the key needed to be in the keyhole to open the front door from the inside. Yet, for a brief while, Jonathan had appreciated how the visitors reflected his new life. Over bottles of sparkling Prosecco shared in outdoor *trattorias* overlooking gushy baroque fountains, all the bright vacationing faces reassured him and Fiona that they were living out a dream. "Move back?" barked one of Jonathan's sister's friends, when Fiona mused about the possibility. "To eight-lane highways, strip malls and doughnut shops on every corner? Why would you even *contemplate* moving back?" Why, indeed? Jonathan raised his glass and *cincin*-ed their transitory companions.

Fiona had landed them in the dream. Top marks in urban planning and rave recommendations from her profs snagged her a job at a prestigious international historical preservation foundation based in Rome. Jonathan, halfway through a floundering thesis on the fifth-century invasions that led to the fall of Rome, from the Goths to the Vandals to the collapse of the western empire, saw it as a sign. Screw the degree; here was a chance to convert his expertise in downfall into cash. He designed a crash course in ancient history, a three-stop ambulatory tour of the Roman empire—from monument to wine bar to ruin—that proved to be a winner with the Americans. True, it would take time to reach a more exclusive clientele (people, for instance, who could read Roman numerals); but when he wasn't escorting herds of retirees from Nebraska over the jagged terrain of the Forum, he sat in his closet-cum-office wedding his research to a cheap, heart-thumping plot.

Jonathan was writing a historical thriller.

At least that was the plan. After nine months of procrastinating, Fiona pointed out that he hadn't actually done any writing.

"It's the guests," he said. "I can't concentrate with all the guests. They're like an invasion."

"Then raise the drawbridge. Stop saying they can come."

So, when the last of the second round of fall season guests—a joyless honeymoon couple from Winnipeg (friends of Jonathan's mother's hairdresser) who broke the kitchen shutters and made a solemn production of offering to pay half—finally left, Jonathan saluted them with a soldier's hand raised to the temple. He turned to Fiona and said, "That was the last of the Mohicans. Shoot me if I let another one through this door."

Jonathan got home an hour later with the cheapest screw-top bottle of *vino da tavola* he could lay his hands on. He opened the door and nearly tripped over a duffel bag the size of a small hippo.

"Oh shit, you OK?" he heard a weak, raspy voice ask from the living room.

A long female body was draped over the sofa, the details of her face blurred by a haze of cigarette smoke.

"Hey there," she croaked. "You must be Jonathan."

"That's right." He jingled his keys. "And you must be ... "

"Cressida." She sat up halfway, as if the whole way would take too much energy, and reached out a skinny arm that tinkled with bangles. Jonathan shook her hand. She was pale with limp blond hair and a lopsided grin that shot up her face like a crack. He estimated her to be anywhere between thirty and fifty. An aggressive wave of musk lifted off her, and he sneezed.

"Sorry about the smoke," Cressida said, fluttering a hand in the air and flopping back into the cushions. "I wouldn't dream of smoking in someone else's space, but I was so freaked out that Fiona told me to just go ahead." A saucer sat beside her on the floor, spilling butts and ashes.

"Did she." Jonathan moved past her and manoeuvred open the window. A weak advance of evening air edged into the room.

"Yeah. Thank fucking God for Fiona. I'd be lying on the bathroom floor of the restaurant with my wrists slit if she hadn't answered the phone and ordered me to take a cab to your place *that second*. The crazy fucker of a cab driver followed me all the way up here, screaming in Italian. As if I'm going to pull a ride-and-run dragging *that!*" She jabbed her cigarette in the direction of her duffel bag. "But Fiona was great. She took care of everything."

"Really."

"Yeah," Cressida inhaled and blew out. "She's a goddess."

"Where's the goddess now?"

"Shower." Then she held up an empty wine glass and flashed her grin. "Hey, mind if I have some of that red stuff? The last bottle was like having my throat rubbed with velvet. Wow."

Fiona padded barefoot into the room wearing a bathrobe, her hair wrapped in a towel. She was small and pale with freckles and smooth, even features. Even wrapped in terry cloth she had the effect she always had on Jonathan: disarming.

"Hi," she said. "So you two have met?" She chewed on the inside of her cheek.

"Oh yeah," said Cressida. "We were just talking about how great you are." She turned back to Jonathan, "Hey! Wine!"

"Go for it," Jonathan said, handing her the bottle. He turned to Fiona. "Sooo?"

"So," said Fiona, her eyes moving carefully across the floor. "So, Cressida's had a rather odd thing happen to her."

"That's one way of putting it," said Cressida, who was pouring red wine above their beige sofa with dangerous verve. "Outrageously fucking cowardly is another."

"She was supposed to meet up with her boyfriend," explained Fiona.

"Fiancé," corrected Cressida.

"Yes. And, well, things took a strange turn."

"Stood up?" asked Jonathan.

Fiona nodded, but Cressida shook her head vigorously. To Jonathan's mixed relief and concern, she drained her glass without spilling a drop.

"No. That's the thing," she said, when she came up for air. "We *met*. We had lunch. We totally hit it off. I mean, you can tell when the chemistry isn't there. I've faked that enough for one lifetime. But we practically had our hands down each other's pants. And then, halfway through lunch, he gets a call on his cell and says he's got to step outside to take it."

"Uh-huh," said Jonathan. "And then … ?"

"And then nothing."

"He didn't come back," said Fiona. "And Cressida doesn't have his cell number here."

"Oh."

Cressida pressed her lips together, blinked and then burped.

"How long did you wait?" asked Jonathan.

"Four hours."

"Oh."

"You know," said Fiona, in a breathy voice, "I had a

thought while I was in the shower. Rome is such a confusing city. Maybe he wandered away from the restaurant—got so engrossed in the telephone conversation that he got turned around. And couldn't find the restaurant again."

"I thought of that too," said Cressida. "Except that he took his bag with him and his map was in it. I thought it must be what you do in Italy, you know, with all the pickpockets. And then, he was the one who booked the restaurant. He set up the whole week. He gets all these great deals, being in the hospitality industry, so it was practically free anyway. Four stars all the way."

"I'm confused," said Jonathan. "This is your fiancé? But it was your first time meeting?"

"Internet," murmured Fiona.

"What?"

"They met on the Internet. This was their first in-person encounter."

"*Oooh*," Jonathan said. "I get it."

"You don't have to say it like that," said Cressida. "It's not like he made shit up. Believe me, I Googled the hell out of him. He was for real. We talked on the phone daily."

"In English?"

"No, in Swedish. Duh, of course in English. He's from Buffalo."

"Buffalo. As in New York?"

"They met in Italy because they wanted the first time together to be … romantic," explained Fiona.

Cressida nodded. "Yeah, romantic, memorable. All that bullshit. He put an ad in the paper and what can I say, I fell hook, line and sinker." She groped the floor for her handbag, fished out a piece of paper and handed it to them.

Saving Rome for Someone Special

She walks in beauty, in a trance
In quest of romance far from home.
He's been to London, wandered France;
For someone special, he's saving Rome
To eat and drink, at night to dance.
For a love that lasts, email or phone.

"Catchy," said Jonathan. "Shame about Rome/phone. So near and yet so far."

"Isn't that Byron?" Fiona asked. "She walks in beauty?"

Cressida sat up. "I can't believe you got that. It's my favorite poem. It's what got me." She twisted a fist on top of her heart. "I thought, OK, this one's meant for me. Even if I hate travelling."

She poured herself another glass of wine.

Jonathan decided it was the moment to graciously bow out. "If you'll excuse me, I'm going to walk in beauty into the closet. Work to do."

"He's writing a book," said Fiona. "Set in ancient Rome."

"Wow, cool. Can't wait to read it," said Cressida. She blew a kiss across the room. "You're the best. You two saved my life."

The next day, after peeling herself off their couch in late morning, monopolizing the bathroom for an hour and burning the handle of their espresso pot, Cressida finally left with Fiona for the bank machine and travel agency. They returned fifteen minutes later with no money (her debit card had failed) and the knowledge that the ticket Mr. Vanished Ex-Fiancé had finagled out of the airline at extremely low cost was locked in. She had a week to go in the Eternal City. Fiona handed her a hundred euros.

"Thanks. And don't worry about me," she said, sinking back on the couch. "I can sleep anywhere. I once slept on a guy's balcony for a month, but don't get me started on that one."

Jonathan didn't. Instead, he sat at his computer and pulled up the email from Jeffers:

Hey Fi,

How's my fave sister?? How's la dolce vita??! I will make it there one of these days ... been SWAMPED with the band ... Anyways, got a tiny favour to ask. Mitch, bass player (who says hi by the way, and who's STILL totally mortified about throwing up on you that time), his ex is going to Rome to meet up with some guy and he asked for your number to give to her so you could get together for a drink or something. He kind of owes her big time. (Lo-ong story.) But NO OBLIGATION. I know you guys are busy with all that cultural shit you do but she's got your number and may call. I underline MAY. She's fun, kinda wacky, but totally cool. You'll love her. Anyways ... huge hug and give Jonty one of those cheesy Italian cheek twists. And tell him to be good to my one and only sis or I'll come after him with a shotgun!!! Just joshing.

Luv u guys,
Jeffers

Jonathan emailed Jeffers a terse rundown of the situation.

That night in bed, Fiona said, "She really did have a horrible thing happen to her."

"Horrible and humiliating. And may I add *unbelievably dumb*."

"Well, I suppose she could have thought things through more ... "

"No money for a hotel in case Mr. Internet Romance didn't show? Nary a credit card?"

"Not everybody has a credit card."

"No, Fiona. *Everybody* has a credit card. Six-year-olds with police records have credit cards."

"He promised her love. Everyone's lookin' for love." She draped her leg over Jonathan's.

"Ah yes, a cyber-promise." He mimed a flourish of hammering above his head. "Chiselled in air."

After they turned out the light, she said, "You know, you can say what you want about her, but I kind of admire her guts. She just puts herself out there. Says what she thinks."

"I want her gone."

He needed to concentrate. After a prolonged bout of writer's block, he was making progress. Once the last guest had cleared out, the first hundred pages had come in an almost obscene rush, *furor loquendi* bordering on logorrhea. Then chapter five had slammed shut like an iron gate. Behind it, he had equivocated, retreated into research, lunged with a flurry of words, deleted them, masturbated. In his cramped cell of creative void, anxieties had scurried like rats. He'd worried about the book: that he wouldn't finish it. He'd worried about his tours not taking off. He'd worried about the condition of his gums, which appeared to be receding. He'd worried about Fiona wanting to move back. He'd worried that this whole stab at Rome just might turn out to be, *in breve,* a monumental failure.

Then after months of captivity, the gate had creaked open and the words began to come. A slow, measured march toward completion. He needed to stay focused. He needed space. He needed quiet. He did not need a jilted boozer named after an obsolete Toyota idling outside his door.

By Sunday Cressida had taken over the entire living room. With her duffel bag spewing clothing like entrails and empty wine bottles lying around like evidence, she'd managed to make their one communal relaxation space resemble a crime scene. She left the couch only to transfer her body to the window, where Fiona had asked her to smoke because the smell was making her sick, or to occupy the bathroom or to eat in the kitchen. At meal times she nibbled on prosciutto and fried eggs, refusing pasta outright. "It's a carb bomb. Totally screws with my mood," she said. ("A car bomb," Jonathan heard at first.)

In the afternoon, Fiona, looking worried, left to catch up on some work at her office. Jonathan sat in front of his computer, cruising dental sites. Cressida lay on the couch, sighing as she flipped through pages of poems by Byron, Keats and Shelley—"her guys." She kept their cordless phone on her lap.

"I've got this really weird feeling he's gonna call," she explained, when Jonathan got up to go to the bathroom.

"Who? The guy who left you in the restaurant?"

Cressida narrowed her eyes until they were two puffy slits. "What is *with* you?" she said. "Do you get some kind of sick pleasure out of rubbing this in my face? *Do you?*"

166

"No. I merely wasn't aware he had our number. I—"

"He's got it, OK? Now don't you have some … "—she made quotation marks with her fingers and wiggled them—" … some *'writing'* to do?"

That night, Jeffers emailed back, "a LITTLE concerned," alluding to "a few issues" he hadn't been totally aware of with Cressida, and that "it might be a good idea to let her crash at your place till she gets on the plane. Mitch HIGHLY recommends it and says he owes you BIG TIME."

Jonathan wrote back, in the most neutral language he could marshal, that Cressida was not working out as their guest. "I'd be grateful if you and your buddy who now owes both me and her **big time** figured out a way to get her home. **Pronto.**"

He did his best to avoid Cressida on Monday. In the morning, he emerged from the bedroom as late as he could, only to have to wait fifteen minutes for her to finish in the bathroom. He rushed off to his ten-thirty—a church group from Florida whom he took through the catacombs and was careful not to disabuse of their cherished belief that persecuted Christians had hidden in the underground graves. Tips were good; mission accomplished. For lunch, he zipped over to Campo de' Fiori, picked up some vegetables and *mozzarella di bufala* for later and stuffed his face on a plate of carb-loaded *penne alla carbonara*. When he got back to put in a few hours of writing, Cressida was snoring.

He slipped into his office and went to get online. And couldn't. He noticed the modem was unplugged. He plugged it in and tried again. No luck. He emerged from the closet, stood at the end of the couch and said, "Cressida."

Her eyes sprang open. "I was sleeping. What?"

"Did you use my computer, perchance?"

"Oh, yeah," she groaned. "I had to check my email. But it didn't work, so I gave up."

"Curious. Because it doesn't work for me now either. Did you unplug anything? Perchance?"

"I dunno. Might have."

"Any chance of remembering clearly?"

Cressida bolted upright. "Look, back off, will you? If I broke something, just tell me. It's not like I won't pay for it." She slumped back down. "I was *sleeping*."

That night, Jonathan fastened a small padlock to the closet door.

On Tuesday, after three hours at the computer repair shop having his laptop inspected and the modem replaced, Jonathan motored to the Domus Aurea, where he walked a group of Texans through Nero and the Great Fire of Rome. When he got back, Cressida was on the couch talking on the phone. Empty Coke bottles littered the floor.

She covered the phone with her hand and said, "Fiona said it was OK to make some calls. Just send me the bill when it rolls in."

He entered his closet and tried to write.

"I know, I know, I know. Tell me about it ... " he heard Cressida say, with minor variations, for an hour. "Yeah, I'll get through it ... Shit happens ... What doesn't kill you makes you stronger ... May he rot in hell, that's what I say ... "

Jonathan exited the closet. "I'm having a hard time concentrating in here. Maybe it's time to give the phone a rest."

Cressida had been applying polish to her toenails as she talked and cotton balls sprouted from between her toes like bunny tails. She put her hand over the phone. "I'll be off in a sec."

"Super. I'll wait."

She turned away from him and whispered into the phone.

Jonathan moved closer. "Hang up now. Please."

"Man, *someone's* uptight."

"Give me the phone." He reached out to grab it, but Cressida swung her arm away. "*Whoa!* Take it easy, elephant ears."

"What did you call me?"

"Things just got extremely tense here," she grumbled into the phone. "*Him.* I'll call you later."

She pressed the off button and handed the phone to Jonathan. Slowly. "Anger management problem or what? I see Fiona's point."

When Fiona got home, Jonathan ushered her into the bedroom.

"What have you been telling her about me?"

"Nothing."

"You've had no talks about me?"

"No. Take it easy."

Jonathan paced along the bed. "I want her gone tomorrow."

Fiona shook her head. "Look, we can't do that. She leaves on Friday—just a couple more days. I talked to Jeffers today and she has some serious issues."

"Speak English."

"She's been suicidal. And, well, she's told me some things."

"Like what?"

"Nothing too specific. Vague death fantasies set in

ancient Rome. She mentioned them to me her first night here, when she was so distraught."

"Vague death fantasies set in ancient Rome? That should be doable. Cinecittà should have some old sets lying around."

"Jonathan, she's on medication. She's ... not well."

"No, she's not. She's sick. A sociopath. And like all sociopaths, she knows how to wrap kind, unsuspecting people around her little finger. Believe me, she's bent on destruction. Divide and conquer."

"Who?"

"Us."

Fiona sighed. "Do you have to speak in war metaphors all the time? It's creepy. All that battle stuff—it's getting to you."

Jonathan *had* been reading a lot of battle material lately. More than usual. A very exclusive outfit, Erudite Tours based in New York City, *la crème de la crème* of walking tour companies, had contacted him on the recommendation of someone who had been very impressed with his Fall of Rome. They wanted to try him out on the 1527 Sack. Not his era, but he brushed up on anecdotes of condemning the Vatican—Pope Clement VII holed up safely in Castel Sant'Angelo while the rest of Rome was raped and pillaged. Given the current popularity of priests in the US, a guaranteed crowd-pleaser.

When Jonathan got up the next morning, the apartment was tomb-silent: the couch was Cressida-less and there was no sign of her in the kitchen or bathroom. Gone at last, he thought, until he spotted a skewed heap of dresses and belts and beads in the corner of the living room. Correction: out. Good enough.

He relished his coffee in silence, his shower without bracing for the sudden end of the hot water and full frontal nudity in the bedroom with the door wide open. He wiggled his hips and jiggled his balls, because he could.

At ten-thirty he went to leave. And couldn't.

The door had been locked from the outside and the key necessary to unlock it from the inside—the key they *always* left in the keyhole—was missing. He dug through the key dish. He checked his pockets. He got under the couch and the bed. He tore through Cressida's pile of crap. Then he faced reality: he was locked in. Cressida had gone off with his keys and, upon leaving, had locked him in.

He called Fiona's cell.

"Where's Cressida?"

"I thought you'd be glad she wasn't there," she said in a chipper morning voice. "She was making a big effort to get out before you woke up."

"She locked me in. She took the keys and locked me in. Where the hell is she?"

"She … oh gosh." Fiona's voice lost the cheer. "She was going over to the Protestant cemetery to look at Keats and Shelley's graves."

"She locked me in to go grave-hopping and you 'oh gosh' me?" Jonathan yelled. "I've got the Sack of Rome in twenty minutes."

"Shit."

"You have to come home and let me out. Take a taxi."

"I'm in southern Tuscany today. Remember? The Etruscan ruins?" She lowered her voice. "With my boss."

"SHIT!"

Jonathan tried the landlord, a man consistently unreachable except at the start of the month, and left two messages. Then a third. He did an even more frantic search for keys. He tried picking the lock with one of Cressida's cheap metal bangles that he twisted open and bent. He ran around the apartment, screaming and jumping and pulling on his hair. He stuck his head out the window and considered the four-storey drop. He paced. He whimpered.

Fiona phoned back. "Have you tried the landlord?"

"I'll kill her."

"Breathe."

"Fiona, this was my big breakthrough. *Erudite.* Ten investment bankers and their spouses await me to take them through a day-long, lunch-included walking tour of the most spectacularly traumatic moment in post-medieval Roman history. *You* breathe."

At six p.m., as Jonathan lay splayed across the hallway floor reading a lesbian murder mystery—the only book he could locate that did not have ancient, modern or culinary Rome as its theme and thus could not remind him of where he was and where he *hadn't* been—a key rattled in the door. It took all his self-control not to throttle Cressida as she entered.

"Hey there," she chirped, dumping her bag on the floor and the keys in the dish. "Tell me what an idiot I've been! Hanging around here—waiting for that asshole to call and listening to you moan and punch your keyboard for three days—when I could have been out there." She aimed a thumbs-up at the door. "Wandering around Rome, sucking up history. Down at the Forum, on top of that big white wedding cake thing near where Mussolini gave his speech. This city is fan-fucking-amazing!"

She glided towards the bathroom.

"Why'd you do it?" Jonathan seethed.

"Do what?" A red thong hanging from the lamp caught Cressida's attention. She looked around and spotted the rest of her clothing sprayed around the apartment. "Hey, what the hell happened to my stuff?"

"You locked the door. You locked me in."

"Did you wreck my organization? It took me an hour to get my shit—"

"YOU LOCKED ME IN!"

Cressida started, looking at Jonathan like he was a small but potentially dangerous animal. "No, I took the spare keys."

"No. No, you didn't," Jonathan said, adopting a soft monotone that freaked even him out. "There are no spare keys. A former guest lost them. You took my only key and you shoved it in the door from the outside and you turned it and then you went off to drool over buried corpses and left me *locked in*."

Cressida lifted a ring of keys from the dish and dangled them next to Jonathan's against her nose. "I coulda sworn they were the same."

"Those are the keys to Fiona's office, which she didn't need today because she's in Tuscany. Far, far away."

"Oh shit. So, like, you've been locked in here all day?"

He snarled.

She backed away, then crossed her arms. "Did you at least get some writing done?"

"NO I DIDN'T GET ANY WRITING DONE!" His feet performed a horrifying jig of rage. "I had the Sack of Rome today. The Sack of fucking Rome, for the most prestigious fucking tour group in the world and I was stuck in here with your beads and bangles and pantyhose!"

He leapt to snatch the red thong off the lamp, but Cressida's arm shot out and nabbed it first. She held it above her head and backed away.

"I'm not taking this abuse." She side-shuffled, then scurried toward the bathroom.

"Don't take it!" he yelled, following her. "Please don't take it. Leave!"

"You're a crazy bastard," Cressida hissed, diving in the bathroom and locking the door. From behind it, she shouted, "Jeffers warned me you were a prick, but he was wrong. You're not a prick. You're the Roman Emperor of pricks. You're Prick Caesar."

"You got it!" Jonathan cackled. "And Prick Caesar commands you to leave!"

"You can't force me. Fiona wants me here. I'm a breath of fresh air. *Her* words."

Jonathan marched back into the living room and snatched Cressida's clothing off the bookshelves and lamps and window knobs. He stuffed fistfuls of Cressida paraphernalia in her duffel bag, crying, "All Hail Prick Caesar!" and "*Ave Cesare Prickus!*"

When the bag was near full he looked up to see Fiona standing in front of him, flushed. "What's going on?" she asked.

"She's out of here. Now," he said, shoving a sequined miniskirt into the bag.

Fiona walked down the hall to the bathroom, from which Cressida wailed, "Where the hell is my medication?"

Fiona tapped on the door. "It's me, Cressida. Please open up."

The door flung open and Cressida, face bloated with tears and rage, swung around to face Jonathan. "Where are they? Where are my pills?"

A smile spread across his face. "They're yours when you leave."

Cressida moved toward him. "I'm going to kill you."

Jonathan chuckled. "Me? What happened to your plan to kill yourself? Your plunge off the Palatine Hill into Circus Maximus? Or was that too logistically complicated? Finding the right bus, buying a ticket."

Cressida turned to Fiona. "You told him? You told this *barbarian*?"

"I was worried," said Fiona. "I was very, very worried."

"Actually, Cressida, you should be aware that the original Greek meaning of 'barbarian' is 'foreigner.' Technically, we're both barbarians, baby."

Cressida's face contorted. "You never stop, do you? *On and on.* Just like your book. Pretentious and rambling and monotonous."

"You read my book?"

"Yeah, like you didn't want me to?" Cressida stuck her finger in her cheek and tilted her head. "Like, ooops, I'm in such a big fat rush to get to my tour that I forgot to shut the closet door and turn off the computer and close my file with the title in big, bold letters across the screen. *Saving Rome by Jonathan R. Whiteside.* Gee willikers! I didn't mean for anyone to actually read it."

"You *read* it."

"I could barely get past the first chapters, but I kept *slogging* away. Just when I thought it couldn't get any more full of clichés and nauseating sex scenes—'She slid onto his sword like a well-oiled sheath.' *Barf!*—then I get to chapter five. BORING!"

"Stop, Cressida," said Fiona. "Stop."

"And that preposterous premise that one battle could save Rome. Any bozo who's read a guidebook knows that Rome was coming apart at the seams by the time the Vandals got there."

"It's fiction!" he screamed.

"Oh no, it's not," Cressida snapped. "It's *prick*tion.*"

Jonathan headed to the corner of the living room, where he hefted her duffel bag onto his shoulder. He hauled it to the window, glanced down, then shoved it out. A thud sounded from below. He stomped to the bedroom and reappeared holding a bag of medicine bottles. "Want your pills?" he said, holding them up and shaking the bag. "Want 'em?"

"Jonathan, for God's sake, just give them back to her," said Fiona. "Let's all calm down. Let's just *calm down.*"

Jonathan walked to the window and dangled the bag. A voice called from below. "Better get moving if you want to sleep tonight," Jonathan said, and released the bag. A musical clattering rang out.

Cressida stood blinking at Jonathan, then began moving toward him, her arms rising, readying for attack. But the voice called out again and she stopped, then headed toward the front door. She was almost through when she turned and put a hand on one hip, thrusting it out. "All I can say is you two turned out to be major disappointments." She pointed at Jonathan and scoffed, "And good luck with *him.*"

A month later, following an afternoon of Christians and Lions at the Coliseum, Jonathan came home to find Fiona sitting at the table, holding an envelope.

"What's that?"

"The money Cressida owed us." She raised her eyes. "She dropped it off."

Since the night of her departure, neither he nor Fiona had breathed the Cressida name. When Fiona came home from work each day, Jonathan would disappear into the closet, materializing for dinner and bedtime, conversing with Fiona in the careful way of the shell-shocked. The recovery strategy Jonathan chose was suppression. Not to think about or discuss what had happened. He allowed himself only one pleasurable fantasy, in which the person in question, drugged and boozed up, mid-Atlantic on her flight home, leaned on the emergency exit handle while on her way to the washroom and got sucked out of the plane, bangles and all, gone forever. That she was alive and still in Rome was not something he had considered.

"She met someone," Fiona said.

"What do you mean, 'met'?"

"The night you kicked her out, she ended up at that Celtic bar and met a man. A Roman. They're getting married."

This seemed not only outside the realm of possibility, but far beyond the conjecture zone surrounding it. "This is bullshit," he said.

Fiona shook her head. "No. He came by with her today. They seemed smitten. He lit her cigarette."

"You let her smoke?"

"In the hallway, as they were leaving."

Jonathan paused to absorb this information. "Now tell me, what kind of human being would marry Cressida?"

"This may sound odd, but he reminded me of those men on the Forza Italia election posters. You know, double-breasted suit and perfect hair. Smarmy, but kind of take-command."

"A neo-Fascist. She's found a neo-Fascist boyfriend."

"Fiancé."

This struck them as incredibly funny and they bent over the table and laughed until tears streamed down their faces. Jonathan threw himself at the laughter like it was the lifeline that would rescue him and Fiona from this impasse. He laughed and laughed until he realized that the gut-wrenching, heaving motion his body was undergoing wasn't laughter, but sobbing.

"She was right," he cried, sliding off his chair onto the floor. "That fucking psycho bitch was right. My novel was unreadable. Garbage."

"Not everyone can write a thriller."

"No, Fiona, anyone can write a thriller. Only *I* can't."

She crouched down beside him and turned his head to look at her. At her stern, sensible, beautiful gaze. "I'm going home," she said.

"Oh God. Ohgodohgodohgodohgod," he moaned, shutting his eyes. "Nooo. Anything but that. Get me out of this nightmare … "

"I'm pregnant."

He opened his eyes. "Since when?"

"Since two months."

He pulled himself upright, did some basic math. "Did *she* know?"

"She saw me throwing up."

Jonathan groaned. "She noticed and I didn't." He pulled up his knees and wailed some more.

"Snap out of it."

He stopped.

"I'm tired of this," said Fiona. "I want to start my life."

He peered up at her. "With me?" he asked, hearing what a pathetic little squeak that question made.

"I'm trying to figure that out. I was hoping that coming to Rome was what you needed. To pull you out of your rut. But you're still in there. Only now there are pretty ruins in the background."

"But I'm trying. What else can I do?"

"Get a grip on yourself. Finish off the PhD. Get a job. Whatever. Just stop being such a self-involved … prick."

"But that's who I am. I'm Prick Caesar."

The corners of Fiona's mouth twitched, then turned down. "Oh, Jonathan, grow up will you?"

As he watched Fiona stand and begin dinner, calmly pulling out bowls and pots and chopping vegetables, it dawned on him that he really hadn't had a clue about defeat. That there was no crashing thrill of disaster, no exhilarating final blow. Only the realization that the center of something he thought would always be there had shifted away. And that the only way he might ever win it back would mean facing the fact that Rome, as he'd imagined it, was lost.

Romeo Gone

WHEN AGNES BLAIS DISCOVERED THE HOLE under the fence, a wave of despair washed over her. She grasped the fence post for support.

"Romeo!" she called over the fence. "Romeo! Come!"

She lowered herself to her knees, a painful manoeuvre at her age and with arthritic hips, and shifted her weight onto her hands to inspect the hole. There was no doubt about it: it was just wide enough for his miniature mongrel body to squeeze through.

He must have waited, she thought. He must have waited until I was in the bath.

With no warning, Agnes's elbow gave out and her cheek went colliding into the fresh mound of earth that Romeo had kicked up before trotting off freedom's way. She hauled herself back onto her hands and then up on her feet. Still trembling, she fixed her eyes on the gap, from above.

"Your face is all dirty."

It was Taylor, or Tyler; Agnes could never remember which. The boy next door, whom she'd spied earlier looping endlessly around his back patio on a skateboard.

"Romeo got away," she said, brushing her cheek with the back of her hand. "You haven't seen him, have you?"

"No," replied the boy. He lived with his father, who never seemed to be around. He scrunched his face up and squinted down the back lane. "Maybe he's in someone's garage. At our old house, our cat got stuck in a garage for two weeks."

"Christ."

"She almost starved to death. Her skin got, like, all saggy. We had to put her on this special diet and everything. And, like, right after, she got creamed by a car."

The boy stood with his mouth hanging open, waiting for Agnes to respond. She muttered another, weaker, "Christ."

What Agnes would've said, had she been in a better frame of mind—what she later wished she had said—was that Romeo wasn't some trampy feline who went snooping in people's garages and sashaying into traffic. Romeo was far too swift and happy a dog to swap his secure existence for adventure. But she was too discouraged to say anything. Instead, she called Romeo's name over the back fence. Then she pushed through her back door and out the front and made her way to the intersection at the end of her street, where she stood squinting into the hostile dazzle of late-morning traffic. Romeo wouldn't survive a second out there. She shouted his name some more, but could hardly hear her own voice above the din of cars. Light-headed and with her hips throbbing, she turned for home.

Back in her yard, Agnes eased herself into the lawn chair behind the spray of forsythia, safe from the boy's brassy intrusions. Her stomach was bothering her, like there was something in it she just couldn't digest, which was strange because she'd lost her appetite lately and had hardly eaten a thing in days. And now this. Romeo gone!

She lit a cigarette, inhaled deeply and cried. She wished she were on speaking terms with Charmane. The girl was good in emergencies, level-headed and able to put emotion on hold, even if asking Charmane for anything always came with a price tag. She'd been downright surly with Agnes for years. It had started just before her sixteenth birthday, when she began calling her "Mother" instead of Mom. "Yes, *Mother*, I heard you, *Mother*," like she was mocking her. Then she took to pointing out that she was old enough to leave home legally. Agnes didn't like being threatened, didn't like the way it made her stiff and tipsy at the same time. But she didn't let Charmane know that. Lord no! The girl had enough of the upper hand already. Agnes played it cool: "There's the door. It's wide open. You can march out into the big wide world any time you like." When she did just that at seventeen and one month and didn't return, not even to pick up the bag of clothes that Agnes had put out on the porch and then threatened to drop off at the Sally Ann, it was like the girl had gone off with a part of Agnes herself. Her optimistic, carefree part. For a while, she allowed herself a little fantasy: Charmane would return and there'd be a tearful reconciliation and they'd be like two girlfriends sharing a place. But eventually she'd had to face the fact that Charmane wasn't coming back, and Agnes had hardened herself around the loss.

It was noon now and the sun glared bluntly at the small patch of grass that had been Romeo's terrain. The elastic of Agnes's sleeves dug into her upper arms, which had swelled in the humidity. She hauled herself up off the chair, too beaten to fold it, and went into the house. She took two extra-strength painkillers and lay on the bed, blinds down, the industrial drone of the small window AC unit blocking out any sounds from beyond the walls. She needed a little rest to gather her strength, so she could think more clearly. But her mind leapt and jerked, anxiety plunging though her like a reckless teenager on one of those bungee cords. She shifted around trying to ease the tightness in her stomach, which wouldn't go away. She'd finally taken herself off to the doctor's last week to have some tests. Probably nothing, he'd said; probably just a bug. His secretary had left three messages asking Agnes to call back, but she couldn't bring herself to do it. Not yet.

Terry would've ribbed her about avoiding the secretary's calls like that. If he'd been good for one thing, it was poking fun at her worry—jabbing a little hole in her view of things just big enough to make her see how carried away she could get. Problem was, he'd also known just what button to push to send her over the top. As Agnes had said when she called in to a radio talk show about battered wife syndrome back when it was all the rage, everyone has an invisible line. Someone pushes you over it, well, there's no holding you responsible for what follows, is there then? She'd been thinking of the last fight with Terry. The cast-iron pan had only grazed his head and he'd come back with a slap across her face, but she'd hardly felt it. All those endorphins and whatnot charging through her body. She was so infuriated that she kneed him in the groin, and when he crumpled to the floor, wailing like a coyote, it just enraged her more. So weak! She called a taxi and sent him off to his brother's across town. She'd seen him only once after that, at their granddaughter Candice's baptism. She'd ignored him, mostly, though he spied her sneaking a look at him once and snickered as if he'd caught her with her pants down. For the longest time after he died, a year later of lung cancer, Agnes could hear his low cackle in the scrape of a chair or the rumble of the furnace and wondered if she was losing it.

The sound of her own cry awoke Agnes several hours later. She'd been dreaming of protesters. Dog marchers. In the dream, Terry was a Doberman leading a march down her street, barking obnoxiously to other dogs to join him in his uprising or whatever it was. (Which was a laugh and a half, because Terry had always griped about paying union dues, even when he'd been off with a foot injury he'd gotten falling down the stairs at home and the guys'd fought to get him put on disability.) Agnes was afraid the protest was against her, heading to her house, and she ducked behind her living-room curtains. But the dogs streamed past the bungalow and, as they did, she spotted Romeo. Agnes knew that he'd only accidentally landed among the rabble-rousers. From his thin, scratchy bark, she could tell he was struggling to get back to her. She banged her fists on the window to get his attention, but then it wasn't Romeo at all, but Ray, her son, as a boy. Lost. She tried calling out to him, but her voice seized. All she could do was flap her arms helplessly behind the pane, trying to catch his attention.

She hauled herself out of bed, dabbed a cold facecloth over her eyes and drank some water. Her mouth was parched. She went into the kitchen and made some tea, the only thing her stomach could handle.

After checking the front and back of the house for Romeo, Agnes sat down at the kitchen table, picked up her address book and magnifying glass and looked for Ray's number. He had a whole page to himself, a long list of crossed-out numbers. She hadn't spoken with him since he'd moved up north, trailing after a lady he'd met when his last live-in situation hit the skids. He was always trying to please some female, always adjusting his life to hers like he was afraid that if he didn't, that'd be it. Which it usually was.

Agnes had kept in touch with his first ex, Brenda, in order to see the little girl, although it had been almost four years now since there'd been regular contact. Candice had been only three when they split. And then—Agnes fought back tears. Such a tiny, trusting thing! Such pretty dark eyes, and the way they looked into hers as the little hands stroked the fleshy skin under Agnes's chin. Agnes let out a sob. Her blood sugar must be all off; it wasn't like her to blubber like this. But just thinking about what Brenda's new boyfriend's scumbag brother did—how was it even physically possible to do *that* to a six-year-old? But it had been done, the damage had been done, to little Candice, so to them all. Brenda blamed Ray for not being there more, for not protecting Candice; Ray blamed himself and moved farther and farther away. When Agnes tried to defend him, to explain why he didn't visit much or why he missed the odd cheque—it only happened now and then!—Brenda blamed Agnes. For the rape of a child!

Agnes counted eleven rings and hung up. Ray must be at work or out somewhere, if he still lived there. And to think how proud he once made her! He'd been a glorious baby and a darling young boy. She had been twenty-six and feeling like she was the last left on the shelf, that her expiry date was coming up fast. It was now or never, she'd said. She and Terry got married just before she started to show. They had the party at the restaurant where Agnes was hostessing (they'd opened it up on Sunday afternoon especially for them). She wore peach taffeta with little peach covered buttons, kid gloves and shoes dyed to match. Martha next door had done her nails and hair, curls nice and tight around the temples so they'd last straight through the week. Terry made it through the reception without getting stinking drunk, an accomplishment back then, and Agnes was satisfied: she had a child on the way and a husband with a steady job. The rest she could handle.

Agnes decided to call the volunteer agency. She hadn't talked to them since the cyclist had knocked her down and she'd sprained her wrist. They'd sent a round of eager-beaver students to do her shopping until she was able to carry bags again. But eventually she'd had enough of the smug pleasure they all seemed to take in helping her. Besides, she'd gotten tired of just getting used to one girl and then having some new one show up.

The usual volunteer co-ordinator answered, Poppy or Piper or some silly P name. Agnes told her about Romeo getting lost. The girl made sympathetic noises and suggested she send someone by to stick up notices around the neighborhood, which wasn't a bad idea. She had a friend in the office, she said, an exchange student who might be able to come.

An hour later a young man knocked on her front door. Agnes almost didn't let him in; he was tall and broad-shouldered, with short-cropped hair, square glasses and a strange little beard, like he couldn't make up his mind whether to grow it or not. He spoke with an accent.

"Good-a day, Madam-a," he said and reached out a hand, which Agnes felt she had no choice but to take. "Pleased to meet you. My name is Emiliano."

"What kind of a name is that? Spanish?"

"E-talian," he said. "I am from E-taly."

He smiled, flashing even, white teeth, and nodded as if being from E-taly was the greatest thing since sliced bread.

She eyed him for a moment. "From Italy, eh? There's a lot of you here now, aren't there?"

"Yes," he kept up the smile. "But I am here only for a few months. To study English." Then he cleared his throat. "Maybe I can come in to write the announcement, no? Of the dog disappeared?"

"Right."

She showed him to the kitchen table and realized she couldn't even offer him a decent cup of coffee; there was only instant. She had to pour him a cup of tea from the lukewarm pot. He added a heap of sugar and asked for some lemon, but she didn't have that either, so he just drank the tea as it was, nodding like he was enjoying it.

She hadn't had a man in her house in ages, and she wished she'd at least had the foresight to run a brush through her hair and put on some lipstick. But, of course, she'd assumed it would be another girl.

He'd brought some paper and tape and a marker, but suggested that Agnes write out what she wanted to say, since his spelling in English wasn't good. But Agnes's writing wasn't what it used to be, so she said she'd print it on a scrap piece of paper and he could do the good copy.

He read it out loud when she was done. "Small, white dog of mixed pedigree gone missing. Answers to the name Romeo. Reward for prompt return."

With his accent it sounded different than she'd intended. Not authoritative, like. All the ups and downs in the way he spoke made it seem more like a poem that didn't rhyme than a notice for a lost animal. He pronounced Romeo, Ro-*may*-o.

"I see he's called Ro-*may*-o," he said, "Like Romeo and Giulietta."

"Except there's just Romeo."

"Maybe *you* are the Giulietta, yes?" he chuckled.

The boy was trying to humor her. To be charming. He had striking, almond-shaped eyes with long black lashes, and likely had a little routine for the girls. A little Latin lover routine.

"Just write," she said, lighting up a cigarette.

He went quiet and focused on the writing, his long, thin fingers moving the marker carefully. He did a good job of spacing and his printing was surprisingly neat. Already he was showing more follow-through than Terry ever had.

"Maybe we put how much is the recompense, no?" Emiliano suggested. "The reward."

"Leave it up in the air."

He nodded and grinned, placing a finger under one eye and tugging down a little, like he was secretly signalling her. "Yes, good idea. We don't specificate on that."

When he had finished writing Agnes's phone number, he gathered up the things and said that he was going back to the volunteer office to photocopy the sheet. He would come by again once the notices were up on telephone poles.

As he was about to leave, she asked, "So where you from in Italy?"

"From Rome."

"Rome, eh?"

"Yes, my family lives there from a long time." He rolled his hand around like he was fanning himself. "Many generations."

"That right."

"Yes."

She cleared her throat. "My brother fought over there. During the war. Fought to *liberate* Rome."

A needle of pain shot across Agnes's chest. She hadn't meant to say it like that, have her voice catch the way it did. She hadn't meant to mention Ray, period. To expose him in front of this young stranger.

Emiliano's eyes lit up. "Ah, yes? Really, it's true? He was in Rome?"

When Agnes didn't say anything back, he asked, "What happened to this brother?"

"He was killed. That's what happened to him."

"Ah, I see," he said, frowning, like he really did see. "Yes, many people died in the war. Terrible."

"Better get those signs up," said Agnes.

When she went into the kitchen and put on the kettle, her hands were shaking. Just a little. It had disconcerted her, having this Emiliano person show up, getting her thinking about Ray again, stirring up the old loss. She'd never stopped missing him, if truth be told. A day hardly went by without her wondering what he would think of one thing or other— what some politician said or some new discovery, some new progress. Since she was a young girl, Ray had been the one she'd looked to for pretty much everything. He had protected her. Shielded her from her father when he got drinking, and never said a word about her lip, which the local doctor had made a mess of trying to fix when she was a baby. Ray never let on he even noticed it. (She'd had it fixed first thing when she moved to Toronto and made some money, and with a good lipstick job you could hardly see it.)

When she was little, he'd take her into town, carry her on his shoulders the whole way, while the Studebaker sat rusting in the yard, with no money for gas. Ray would point to the car and say, "That's called a Bennett buggy, Aggie, after our good-for-nothing prime minister. Don't you ever vote Conservative." And she never had. Every year she sent in her membership money to the Liberals and carried her card in her purse, proof of her loyalty to Ray, to her poor mother, to what they all put up with. She told all this to Charmane, unsnapping her wallet and holding the card up for her to see but not touch. During the Depression, her mother went practically barefoot for four years!, she'd cry, as little Charmane sat silently taking her in, eyes wide. Later Charmane would snap, "Oh, Mother, not again! I've heard it all a million times. *No shoes for four years! No shoes for four years!* You had to tell me every last detail, didn't you? Couldn't spare me anything, could you?" No, Agnes couldn't.

During the war, Ray'd started out as an ordinary gunner in the coast artillery. Then he volunteered for the Canadian paratroops and was picked for an elite squad. The First Special Service Force, they called it. The very strongest men. Half Yanks, half Canadians.

He spent twenty-three days in the snow on the top of a mountain near Rome, pushing Germans off the edge. Yet some British member of parliament had the nerve to call them "D-Day dodgers." As if all the real battles were fought in France! The men later wrote a facetious song, set to the tune of "Lili Marlene."

> *We're the D-Day dodgers here in Italy*
> *Drinking all the* vino, *always on the spree …*

A fellow named Jack from out east, who for years had sent a card at Christmas, told her about it later. About how they melted snow to make coffee. About not being able to change their clothing, not even their socks. How they slept out in the open. About Ray's trench feet. The rot that set in from the cold and the wet and no relief. How they couldn't get him back down the mountain soon enough when he caught pneumonia. How he died up there. At twenty-five. Hollywood later made a movie about the mountain battle, but Agnes didn't have the heart to see it. Jack told her they'd got most of it wrong, anyway.

Jack and the other men made it to Rome early that summer, in '44. In one of his letters, Jack wrote about coming across an ancient Roman aqueduct in some field outside the city and how sorry he'd been that Ray, who'd been a real history buff, wasn't there. What a kick he'd have got, that aqueduct so close you could touch it.

When little Ray had come along, Agnes thought she'd gotten a piece of her brother back. He didn't have his uncle's low laugh or broad forehead, but his hair fell in soft, loose curls down the nape of his neck just the same way, so that from behind she could almost believe it was him. But little Ray never had her brother's resolve, had instead a little streak of weakness that got bigger as he got older. Still, he was a winsome boy.

On Saturday nights, when Terry had gone out to the bar to watch hockey, Agnes would dress up Ray and Charmane in matching outfits and take them down to the restaurant on the lake where they had a band. She worked just as hard as Terry and was damned if she wasn't going to have a good time, too. Ray always resisted going. He'd squirm and kick and grab doughy fistfuls of her breasts until she had to give him a good whack on the head. But it would pass, always did, and off they'd go, the three of them in their matching outfits: sailor tops with blue trim, red skirts for the ladies, red pants for Ray, and black patent leather shoes for all. Of course, Charmane was the most fun to get all dolled up, with her chestnut hair and wide-spaced blue eyes. Angel eyes. Agnes would curl her hair in ringlets, spread blue powder eyeshadow across her fluttery lids and slide a little gloss on her lips. She'd have a pink lady and would order the kids Shirley Temples. Then she'd pull Ray onto the dance floor and the whole place would turn to watch them. She'd taught him how to lead, and the two would glide across the parquet in a smart swoosh of red, white and blue.

She was a snappy dresser then and had Betty Grable legs. Not that she took advantage of it—she was never calculating with regard to men. God knows, she wouldn't have ended up with Terry if she had been. It wasn't until after he left for the third time that she decided she'd had enough of nights alone with Ray and Charmane. She'd slip a couple of TV dinners in the oven and make sure there was ice cream on hand, then leave Ray in charge. She'd sit herself down at her dressing table with a drink and start making up her face. ("War paint," Terry used to joke when they were together. "Yeah, and I sure need it living with you!" she'd crack back, but she knew Terry liked it.) Then she'd pull on her girdle and the outfit she'd laid out. Off she'd go, clutch in hand, to the rattling streetcar that carried her downtown to meet Edith from the restaurant.

Edith and she'd had some good times for a while. Some nights it was just the two of them over a few drinks, laughing about some customer or letting off steam about what went on with the cook or the manager. Sometimes gentlemen would come to their table and ply them with drinks and compliments. Sometimes Agnes met up with them later, in furtive encounters between shifts or when the kids were at school. But they never added up to anything, which was just as well. She knew that trying to stretch a string of afternoons of prodding and groping into a relationship wasn't likely worth the energy.

Then the Saturday nights with Edith ended. Edith came from a Seventh-day Adventist background and, while she didn't go to church anymore, she could get high and mighty. If Agnes ordered one gin fizz extra, Edith would poke her elbow into Agnes's side and say, "Don't you think that'll do it for tonight, old girl?" then tsk-tsk when Agnes ignored her and ordered another. Once Agnes did overdo it a little and landed in the ladies room. Edith stood swaying above her, snidely remarking, "What do the kids call this, kissing the porcelain god?" She took Agnes home in a cab. Then, on Monday, she made her pay back every penny—even for Edith's bus fare home—and she had the cheek to hand her a phone number for Alcoholics Anonymous. The friendship pretty much ended there. A couple months later, the manager opened his own restaurant and asked Edith to work for him, and that was that.

While she waited for Emiliano to return, Agnes fixed herself a rum and Coke. It helped loosen her up a bit, got rid of the lump in her throat. She poured herself another. Then she put a couple chicken pot pies in the oven. She sliced a cucumber and tomato and slid them onto a plate with a dollop of mayonnaise. She probably wouldn't eat much herself, what with her stomach doing strange things, but by the time he got back it would be suppertime and he'd likely be hungry.

Agnes changed into the turquoise pantsuit she used to wear when she and Terry went for ice cream at the lake.

With the weight she'd lost lately, it fit again, and once she put on her face she didn't look half bad. When she came back to the kitchen it had that warm chicken and starch smell of childhood Sunday meals. She opened the back door. Romeo could be nearby and might catch a whiff of cooking.

Emiliano got back, looking flushed and not smiling quite so much.

"Made some supper," Agnes said.

He looked a little surprised, but nodded and said, "Oh, very nice. Thank you very much." Then he asked to make a call.

It was to a girl. Agnes could tell by the tone, soft and ingratiating, someone he was still trying to impress. He told her he'd be late, and then lowered his voice and said something Agnes couldn't hear.

"Supper's ready," she called out, and waited until he said goodbye and hung up.

Emiliano turned out to be a talker, prattling on in his mixed-up English about his family: his father who was a professor, his mother who was a painter of some sort, an older sister who was thirty and still studying. Agnes was glad to have the company. It helped take the edge off her worry about Romeo. And it was good to have a change from all the earnest female listeners the agency sent. Turned out Emiliano was almost twenty-four but still lived at home, which Agnes thought didn't say much for him, but she held her tongue and made out like she thought it was all just fine.

"Not hungry?" Agnes asked. He'd hardly touched the chicken pie.

"Oh, yes," he said, "I eat very *piano*, very slow." He pretended to grind his jaw around to show her just how slowly. But then she saw him look at his watch and pop the rest in his mouth, washing it down with a gulp of water.

"I got some ice cream in the freezer," Agnes said. But Emiliano shook his head, said he was full, that he must go. He asked to use the bathroom.

On the way back he stopped to look at the picture on the wall just outside the kitchen door. It was of Terry and her and the kids shortly after Charmane's birth. Agnes was still a little heavy, but Terry had his arm around her like it was there on purpose and wore a tolerant grin that made Agnes do a double take each time she saw it.

"Your family," said Emiliano, smiling. "How beautiful." His eyes moved slowly across their faces, like he was piecing together a puzzle.

"That's us." Agnes didn't feel like they were a family, not even back when she'd tried her darnedest to make them one. She'd told herself she'd kept the picture up because the frame was so pretty, made of some rich, shiny wood, cherry or something. But she wondered now why she hadn't taken it down years ago.

"And your brother?" he asked. "The one … "

"There." She pointed farther down the hall, by the front door. Emiliano moved to stand in front of the picture of Ray. It had been taken just before he shipped out on the *Empress of Scotland*. Ray was in uniform and you could see his shoulder flash: USA across the top and Canada down a spearhead. It was her favorite picture of him; not because it was the last or because he was in uniform, but because something about it caught his character. The straightness of his character.

The boy stared at the picture, then shook his head. "A tragedy," he said. "I am against it. The war. I am a *pacifista*."

"A what?"

"Pacifist. How do you say? I am for the peace."

"Peace?"

"Yes. I even don't do the military service in Italy. I objected, you know. I do a ... civil service instead." He was all puffed out, proud.

Agnes opened the front door and stood on the porch.

"I am sure that he will return," he said.

She thought for a moment he meant Ray, that *Ray* would return, and almost cried out her outrage. But he hadn't meant Ray, he'd meant Romeo.

"If he is Italian like his name, he will get hungry and he will run home to his Giulietta," he chuckled, sticking his hands in his pockets.

What on earth did this young man know? Agnes thought. What on earth did he know about Romeo, about her, about the past or the future, what it would or would not bring?

Emiliano leaned forward in a little bow, then reached out his hand. But Agnes was faster this time. She stepped back. "Goodbye," she said, and shut the door before he could say another word.

She woke up the next morning confused by the faint glow in the room. She'd fallen asleep in front of the TV, had flopped on the loveseat. She had a struggle to get herself upright. On the TV some lady with a tall up-do was going on about a ring, trying to get people to call in and buy it. Agnes watched her hair tilt around with her head, looking as if it would topple at any moment. The pain in her stomach twisted.

She went into the kitchen, made a cup of tea and boiled an egg. She shook out two more painkillers and swallowed them with the tea. Out of habit, she began to fill Romeo's bowl and change his water, then caught herself.

If she hadn't seen the hole with her own eyes, she wouldn't have believed he had it in him. Romeo was devoted to her. She'd gotten him as a puppy from the animal welfare people. He was supposed to be for Candice; she'd wanted to surprise the little girl with the dog once the ordeal was over, but Brenda wouldn't hear of it, said it would just make more work for her and Candice was afraid of dogs anyways. It was really just as well; Agnes was at an all-time low and had gotten attached to Romeo. No one else except her brother Ray had been so loving and loyal. She knew he was a dog, that his mind wasn't full of the jumbled motives and emotions people's were; but this made his love more precious. It was pure. And if it weren't for Romeo's cheery bark each morning, for his panting and tail-wagging encouragement when she was barely able to get out of bed some days, she didn't know how she would have made it through. She couldn't go from one room to the next without Romeo trailing behind her, whining for fear he'd be left behind.

Agnes spent an agitated morning checking at the doors and standing on her front walk, asking passersby if they'd seen Romeo. One lady thought she might have, but described the dog as "scruffy." Agnes finally retreated to the cool of her house.

She pulled the phone onto her lap and dialed Charmane's number. She knew Charmane would accuse her of only calling when she needed something, but if you couldn't call then, when could you? It rang four times, then the answering machine kicked in. Agnes hung up.

They hadn't spoken since last fall. Charmane, who was handy at fixing things, had come by to redo the screen on Agnes's back door after Romeo had wrecked it. Afterward they'd had a couple of beers in the living room and seemed to be getting on well enough, although it was always walking on eggshells with Charmane. The girl was no slouch, Agnes had always acknowledged that, and she was doing well for herself. She was telling Agnes about her new, high-up job in computers. Agnes felt her chest strain with happiness for Charmane and she'd meant to tell her how proud she was—would have if the conversation hadn't got derailed. Charmane decided to take offence when Agnes asked her when she was going to get her own place. She'd been living for four years with some woman named Glenna, a tall, stern-looking person at least ten years older, who sometimes came by with Charmane to see Agnes. For the life of her, Agnes could not understand why Charmane still lived with Glenna when she could well afford her own apartment. It was giving the wrong impression, was all Agnes said, like she'd given up, didn't want a family.

"I don't," Charmane replied.

"You say that now, but if you made some effort to meet a fellow, you might change your tune."

"Like a family with a man worked out so well for you, eh, Mother?" Charmane said.

Agnes erupted at that, although later she was puzzled as to why. She'd had a lifetime of Charmane's defiance and knew better than anyone that a man could bring on more problems than he solved. She supposed she was just tired of Charmane thumbing her nose at her every suggestion. But she regretted splashing the last of her beer in Charmane's face, especially since Charmane didn't even give her a chance to calm down, just left without a word.

Agnes began to cry again. If Terry could see her now, she thought, worrying herself sick over a dog, bawling away, what a laugh he'd have! *Good ol' Aggie, can't say I'm surprised. Driven them all away,* he'd snort. But she hadn't—that was the thing—she'd just wanted them to need her. But if they refused to, then what choice did she have? She would not appear pathetic. Nobody would do that to her.

The phone rang. So sudden it startled her out of her tears. It would be Charmane, she thought. It would be Charmane and she would make amends.

She went to pick up the receiver. But at the last second she remembered the doctor's office and let the machine pick it up instead.

"Hello," a sing-song female voice rose from the machine.

Of course it wasn't Charmane. Couldn't be, Agnes realized. She hadn't left her a message.

"I'm calling because I think I've found your dog—"

Agnes picked up. "Romeo."

"Oh, you're there."

"He's called Romeo."

"Yes, right. I think it may be him. He was digging around in our compost. I think he was hungry."

"Oh no!"

"Hey, he's OK. I gave him some cat food. We're cat people ourselves. Had to shut them in the basement, which didn't make them very happy. Romeo's here in the kitchen with me. He's adorable. Happy little guy. Keeps jumping up on my lap."

Agnes made her decision then. She explained about her hips, about the cyclist, about how hard it was to get around. The woman said, of course she would bring Romeo over. Of course. Just as soon as her husband came back with the car.

Agnes hung up and stood by the front door. After an eternity, a station wagon pulled up in front of the house and a heavy blond woman in pink sweatpants stepped out holding Romeo. He lapped at her chin. She laughed, carrying him up the walk and holding him out to Agnes, saying, "Is he always this frisky?"

"That's my Romeo," Agnes said, pulling him against her chest, her heart aching.

She mentioned the reward, but the woman shook her head and made her way back down the front walk, in a hurry, she explained, to pick up her kids.

Agnes carried Romeo into the living room, where she buried her face in his curls, rubbing back and forth, cooing his name. But after a few minutes Romeo wriggled loose and scrambled into the kitchen. Agnes found him standing on his hind legs against the back door, whining to be let out.

"Romeo, get down!"

He let out a thin whimper and sniffed at his food before settling into his blanket in the corner.

Agnes went to her bedroom and made the call from there.

The arrangements were easier than she'd thought. She explained she was a pensioner and that Romeo was no spring chicken and simply too much. It was all too much.

She took a cab down the next day, clasping Romeo tight with her good arm, Ray's old sports bag looped over the other.

It was all done in less than an hour. She had a good cry in the reception area and a nice nurse brought her a cup of tea. On the taxi ride back along the lake, Agnes caught sight of the joggers and cyclists gliding past, their clothes rippling in the wind. There was a little girl who looked just like Charmane at eight or nine, the same sturdy legs, her hair blowing every which way. The same self-reliant look that Agnes had so wished away.

The humidity had finally lifted and the pain in her hips had eased. She had the driver help her to the door with the bag, which was heavier than she had expected. Trevor, the boy from next door, was pretty much through digging. He carried the bag the rest of the way. It wasn't the four feet she'd asked for, but it would do. She handed the boy the ten-dollar bill she'd promised and he headed off.

She managed to push the bag into the hole with her foot. Then she took the shovel and slowly scraped small clumps of earth over it.

She thought about Ray, her brother, and again about that Italian student. She had been trying to figure out what bothered her so much about what he'd said, and now she realized it was the hypocrisy of it. The lack of recognition. As if by being against war, he was saying that it had all been a big mistake. And that all the heartbreak and toil and suffering that went on, to liberate Rome and to win that war, had been a big mistake, too. As if all the men who died needn't have. And as if for all the hard choices people had to make to survive, to keep going, *to simply keep going,* there was always the luxury of a soft option.

She padded around on top of the earth to push it down, then went into the house and made herself another cup of tea. She tried nibbling on a biscuit, but had no appetite. She was tired. Awfully tired.

As she sat sipping her tea and looking out the back window, Agnes couldn't say the little patch of upturned earth at the end of the yard gave her peace of mind. Without Romeo, or worrying about Romeo, everything seemed too quiet. But she thought that, in time, she'd get used to that, too.

Renovations

WHEN MY HUSBAND'S UNCLE DIED at the age of eighty, he left the bulk of his estate to us. It didn't make us rich, but it was enough to check off one item from our wish lists of things we'd do if money dropped from the sky and landed on our doorstep. I had a few things on my list. At the top: taking a year off to live in India, where Giuseppe and I had planned to go on our honeymoon but never made it, because Giuseppe got his first editing job and then Flavia came along. But like a lot of my wishes, which tend to be vague escapism, it lacked practicality. Flavia, who was now seventeen, had her eye on a scholarship to study in Canada or the States, where she wanted to practice law and live in a big suburban home, like my brother in Toronto. She would refuse India point-blank. Dario had just failed his first year of high school and spent most of his time at a bar down the street doing God knows what, convinced he was living the seminal moments of a career in rap music. Taking either of them was not an option.

Giuseppe wanted to renovate. I was happy with the apartment the way it was—lived-in, a little shabby, comfortable. Its layout was awkward, but I'd gotten used to the long walk down the hall from the kitchen to the dining room and the fact that our bedroom could fit two double beds while the living room could hardly hold a couch. We had bought the place fifteen years earlier, when the kids were still small, and apart from adding shelving to hold all the books and clothing and junk we'd accumulated, we hadn't done a thing. But comfortable doesn't seem to be the point of most Italian homes, and Giuseppe had been itching to redo the apartment for ages. With Uncle Federico's little bundle, he now could.

Part of me was pleased to go along with the plan; I was up for anything that made Giuseppe so gung-ho. Work hadn't been going well for several years. He was the editor of a trade magazine on viniculture and had been promised the editorship of a bigger, more prestigious publication in the same company. Then a takeover happened and the new publisher—a rich, former–Communist Party fundraiser, now an apologist for the far-right on talk shows—handed the job to one of his political cronies. There was nothing Giuseppe could do but wait until, if he was lucky, the man moved on. Even then, there were no guarantees.

With the renovations, Giuseppe had something to pour his creative energy into. In the evenings, he sat at the dining-room table with a block of grid paper and sketched out designs in quick, precise strokes with a blue felt-tipped pen. It was a bittersweet pleasure to see him so engrossed, if only after work. Before bed he'd explain to us how he could fit a closet in the front hall or get two bathrooms out of one if we shifted a wall eight centimeters to the south. Dario would glance and nod and say "*fico*" or "cool," then try to get away before Giuseppe launched into the details, which could get tedious. Giuseppe was hurt by his lack of interest and eyed his low-slung jeans or his eyebrow piercing and told him to stand up straight (Dario has inherited both my height and my slouch), which only made Dario want to get away faster. Flavia wasn't any more interested than Dario; in her mind she was already halfway to America. But she was better at pleasing her father, and she'd listen and suggest ways her bedroom might be enlarged. Giuseppe, who pretends to be exasperated with her selfishness, would fiddle around with his plan to comply. Later he'd slip into Dario's room and ask him if he needed any money. Giuseppe can't stand the tension of being on bad terms with anyone.

I first met Giuseppe at a *cineforum,* one of the hundreds of film clubs that formed in Italy in the seventies, popping up in church basements and Socialist Party centers like porcini mushrooms in the fall. You watched some Eastern bloc movie like *The Battleship Potemkin* and after had *il dibattito,* a political discussion that could go on for hours and get very heated. I loved these evenings, though my Italian wasn't good enough for me to contribute much. I'd been travelling around Europe and was about to start my PhD in English literature—at least, that was the plan. But I got pulled into Rome, which at the time was a seductive brew of old-world grace and revolutionary verve, and I began to postpone my trip back.

I come from a family of four kids and am the youngest by eleven years, an afterthought—or less kindly but more accurately, a mistake. I didn't mind: I was the baby and had affection heaped on me from all sides with no expectations. (My parents were genuinely surprised that I planned to go to university, as if they'd assumed I was a permanent home feature.) But I was always too young to be part of the real action in our family and I think, as a result, my whole life I'd had the feeling of showing up just as the party petered out. These meetings were the first time I'd felt like I'd arrived on time—that at last I'd found myself in the thick of things. They were full of people who dropped references to obscure Freudian or Marxist theorists like they were common household cleaning products. Just being there made me feel part of something urgent and transforming.

Giuseppe was one of the *cineforum* organizers. He hardly ever spoke during the post-film discussions, and when he did it was usually to clarify or paraphrase a point that someone was making sloppily, which he did in such an understated way that nobody felt offended. He'd stand at the back during the evening and as everyone finally filed out he'd hand out flyers publicizing the next film. One night, as I took a flyer I read the title out loud and mispronounced a word. Giuseppe corrected me. Then he asked me to say it again and listened as I repeated the title a couple of times until I got it right. He wasn't flirting, which likely would have been the case with anyone else. (Being tall and blond made me a walking target back then.) He was just helping me improve my Italian. At the next *cineforum* I approached him and asked if he'd like to tutor me in Italian in exchange for me teaching him English, and that's how our relationship began.

You'd never guess at Giuseppe's intellectual precision from looking at him. Physically he's your typical southern peasant, though his family is from Reggio Emilia, in the north. He's short and burly with round cheeks and red lips and eyebrows shaped like arrows pointed upwards, which gives him a sprightly look. He's someone you might easily imagine making pizzas for a living, singing snippets of opera while he rolls out the dough. People are constantly getting him wrong—slapping him jovially on the back when they've just met him or calling him Peppe or Peppino, which he hates but would never let on because he's so well-mannered.

My parents couldn't believe I was marrying someone like him. I grew up in the WASP bastion of Victoria, British Columbia, and while it was fine to eat spaghetti and pizza and drink Italian red wine, it wasn't so fine to marry an Italian. If you absolutely had to, then make it a Milanese banker or the heir to a shoe empire, not a peasant look-alike who works for an obscure magazine on "spirits," as my mother quaintly put it.

They'd met Giuseppe only once, when they visited Rome shortly after I got my first teaching job. It was a busy time for me at work, so Giuseppe offered to show them around. He nearly killed himself making sure they had a good time, ferrying them to out-of-the-way historical sites, straining his English to make the ruins resonate with history. In the evenings he sweated over pasta and meat dishes that would complement the bottles of Barolo or Brunello he'd brought up from the cellar, saved for a special occasion. But by then my parents had heard so many horror stories about so-and-so's daughter marrying an Italian only to be reduced to an indentured servant that they didn't trust Giuseppe. They thought he was putting on a show.

"Does he know you don't cook?" my father asked.

"Oh course he knows. He loves cooking."

"He says that now."

"What's that supposed to mean? That he's luring me into marriage with food?"

"It means people think they want one thing at the outset, when what they really want is something different."

The reno was a big deal for Giuseppe. *La casa* was central to his psyche in a way that I couldn't relate to. It represented all the usual things—shelter, a haven, the family nucleus—but it was also a space he could control, give form to and, I suspected, a space he hoped might give new form to the rest of his life. He was keen for me to share in all the decisions, as if each one was a step in a waltz we were dancing together. I dragged my feet, nodding and smiling through meetings with potential contractors as Giuseppe went over the architectural and financial details, but not paying much attention.

When all the estimates were in, Giuseppe pored over his notes with a calculator and his felt-tipped pen, narrowed them down to three and asked my opinion. The only team I could recall was a threesome, two Italians and a Polish guy. He pulled out their estimate and reread it. "They seem too cheap. I don't know how they can do it for this price."

"Then go for the next guy up."

But the next guy up couldn't start for six months and the third one was too expensive. We settled on the trio, who were delighted to get the work.

The men made their appearance on a hot Monday morning in early June. We live in Monti, a neighborhood that until a few decades ago was for the hoi polloi. It presses right up against the ruins of Trajan's Forum and the remains of a towering, ancient stone wall that had been designed to keep the fires that frequently broke out in the poor district of ancient Rome from spreading to the political power center. The streets in Monti are so narrow and crooked that unless you live on the fourth or fifth floor, direct sunlight reaches into your apartment for only a few hours in the morning or late afternoon. Parking is impossible. From that very first morning, honking sounded from the street throughout the day, and one of the workers would regularly thump down the three flights of stairs, cursing under his breath, to move their truck to let some wide vehicle pass.

After one day there was so much plaster dust in the apartment that just walking from the front door to our kitchen made me feel like I'd spent the day erasing chalkboards. Giuseppe had planned things so that the kitchen and bedrooms would remain liveable, separated from the dust and chaos by great cascading plastic sheets. Later we would switch our camp to the finished side of the apartment with its new kitchen, study and living room, while the old kitchen would be made into a bedroom. Dario was in his element, tramping through the confusion in his Doc Martens like a seasoned squatter in some American slum. But after the second day, Flavia announced that she was moving in with her friend Luisa's family until the end of the school year, in six weeks. I was disappointed; I hardly saw her with all the studying she did. But she just glowered.

"This is so typical of you. Renovating at the worst possible time."

"But we had to go with when the workers were available," I protested. "The timing wasn't my decision!"

"*Exactly.* Nothing ever is." She looked around in disgust. "What a mess."

She phoned from Luisa's that night to say she would come by the next day to pick up some books and have lunch— as close to an apology as Flavia got. But I could hear her relief that she was there and not in the chaos with us, especially me. I irritated Flavia: the way I dressed (too much flowing ethnic cotton), my bad Anglo accent in Italian, even the fact that I had left North America, where she was convinced the pulse of the world thumped, and settled in a place where nothing happened and nothing changed. But I sensed that she had a deeper gripe with me that had less to do with my choices and more to do with who I was. Something closer to disappointment.

But Flavia was right; the place was a mess, and one that got progressively worse. Each afternoon when I came home from work, a new wall had been knocked down or stripped or a stretch of floor had been torn up. My comfortable little nest was no more.

Vincenzo was the senior man on the job, an older man whom everyone addressed as Sor Vincenzo, using the quaint Roman alternative to *signore*. He had bristly white hair and wire-framed glasses and showed up each morning in a khaki flak jacket over a clean white T-shirt, looking more like a war correspondent than a contractor. Fabio, the plumber, was a good two decades younger. He had a look of mild tolerance and forbearance, as if he'd learned early that it would be his lot in life to find himself among people who weren't entirely reliable. We later learned from Sor Vincenzo that Fabio's wife suffered from depression and was in and out of the hospital, so that was likely part of it.

When Fabio and Sor Vincenzo weren't conferring about logistics, they were bickering about politics. Sor Vincenzo was a Berlusconi supporter and a card-carrying member of the Alleanza Nazionale, an offspring of the Fascist Party. Fabio despised Berlusconi; his loyalties lay with the working class. When Sor Vincenzo was building a door frame that turned out slightly crooked, Fabio dubbed it "Berlusconi building." When Fabio was slow bringing coffee up from the bar downstairs, Sor Vincenzo would deride him for his Soviet work habits.

During the demolition phase, Sor Vincenzo asked the painter, Vladimir, whom everyone called Miro, to get a head start on the doors, windows and wooden shutters, which hadn't been touched in decades and needed to be sanded and repaired before being repainted. Miro was in his fifties, with silky black hair and small, deep-set, melancholy eyes. He trembled slightly, which made him appear a little cagey. But there was also something obscurely appealing about him, a shimmer of charisma. He would have been handsome if Polish dental care hadn't been so poor. Several teeth were missing and the rest were brown with tobacco stains. He was self-conscious and pulled his lips over them when he talked or smiled. This lent him an air of mystery—or in one of his rare, light moods, of mischief—as if he were holding in a little secret.

The first month, Miro came a couple times a week with a Polish assistant also called Vladimir, whom he called Choo-choo, a mispronunciation of *ciccio*—"What's-your-name" in Italian.

"Choo-choo!" he'd say, like he was shooing away a dog instead of asking for help, "Pass me the brush!" Or "Choo-choo, take the lids off those paint cans and give them a stir!"

Choo-choo was also lightly built, ten or fifteen years younger than Miro, with the same rotten teeth and a round, cautious face. He skirted around the other workers and me, eyes cast down, as if we were obstacles to avoid. Only when Miro addressed him did he come alive.

At first I thought it was an exploitive relationship, with Miro taking advantage of Choo-choo's more recent immigration to use him as a whipping boy. Then, one morning before the others arrived, Miro sent Choo-choo to get coffee from the bar, yelling irritably at him in Polish as he left. Choo-choo came back with the coffee about ten minutes later and handed it to Miro, who was perched near the top of a ladder. Then he disappeared around the corner, where he was prepping the doors. From the kitchen I could see both Choo-choo and Miro. I knew something was up by the way Choo-choo kept poking his head around the corner. Miro finally folded back the tinfoil top of the little plastic espresso cup and tipped it into his mouth. He spit coffee all over the window he'd been trying to separate from the shutter and bellowed what could only have been Polish obscenities. Shaking with suppressed laughter, Choo-choo darted out onto our small terrace before Miro could corner him. Miro slid down the ladder and charged after him. I was worried they might come to blows and was ready to plead with Miro to calm down. He and Choo-choo eyed each other across a door lying flat on a sawhorse. Then Miro's face twitched and burst out into a beautiful, boyish grin.

"*Sale*," he said, turning to me. "I told Choo-choo no sugar in my coffee, so he put salt instead. Little rascal."

He picked up a rag and, still chuckling, wiped the coffee from the window.

Giuseppe followed the progress of the reno with apprehension, like he was caring for a convalescent child, leaving reluctantly, late in the morning, and coming home most days for lunch. From my makeshift office in a corner of the kitchen, I spent afternoons marking student papers and half following what was going on. Sometimes things got animated, like when Sor Vincenzo accidentally broke a pipe when knocking down a wall, and the gushing water made its way out the door and onto the landing below. Giuseppe rushed home to appease our downstairs neighbor, an elderly woman who had never spared me a smile but who seemed to like Giuseppe. Mostly there were only small arguments about how to reposition a radiator or add illegal plumbing or move a window without the condominium manager catching on. Often in the late afternoon I'd make a pot of espresso and have a break with the men. Sor Vincenzo did most of the talking then, usually about his wife and cooking, subjects that had fused together in his mind. Fabio would contribute the odd memory of some great meal he'd eaten, but other than that he never said much, as if talk of anything more serious might lead him back to his problems. Miro was, on the whole, silent, following the conversation with his small, dark eyes. But then, unexpectedly, he'd open up and tell us about his two sons, one studying engineering in California on scholarship and the other finishing high school somewhere in Poland, or share the fact that his wife (or now ex-wife) lived in Pittsburgh, where they'd moved as a couple fifteen years earlier. Miro had stayed only for a year. "Disgusting," he said of the United States. The only personal subject that seemed to cheer him up was the house he was building in the woods where he grew up, somewhere outside Cracow. Once he brought in a photo of himself and another man standing shirtless in front of a half-built A-frame with tall pines surrounding it.

"One, maybe two more years to go here," he said. He cut the air with his hand like a knife. "Then *finito*."

Other than the coffee breaks, he only spoke with me during the day once, when he came into the kitchen for a glass of water. As he was leaving he paused and asked, "What are you doing every day, all day long, behind this curtain?" He shook the plastic sheeting.

"Marking," I explained, mildly pleased that he was interested. "Students' papers."

He lingered, the answer not seeming to satisfy him. Then he nodded and left.

The men also talked politics, which if Miro, who was both anti-Communist *and* anti-Berlusconi, joined in, could take some bizarre turns. Their arguments reminded me of the *cineforum* debates: government corruption, the question of the South, judicial reforms. (How little things had progressed, despite the feeling back then that change was inevitable.) There were a few global topics, too: whether the government let in too many immigrants or too few, whether Muslims posed a threat. Miro wouldn't miss a chance to make some disparaging comment about Albanians or North Africans, but the other two ignored him, for the most part. One day, though, Miro must have said something especially offensive because Fabio, who usually spoke to him in a light, jocular voice, responded with real distaste.

"And who do you think taught them all their tricks, these Albanians you love to hate? The bozo Communist leaders? No. *Us*. The Italians! We're a race of dogs. And so are the Poles."

A deadly silence followed and lasted for the rest of the afternoon. I was worried that Miro might quit or that Fabio would insist to Sor Vincenzo that he go. When Giuseppe came home from work, he realized something had happened and fussed around the apartment double-checking the placement of the outlets and switches, getting in everyone's way. Finally he went down to the cellar and came back with a bottle of rare vermouth, insisting everyone have a glass. They did, and then had a second. Miro had a third. After his fourth he placed his glass carefully on the tray. Then he rolled his eyes back, tilted his head to the ceiling and howled. An anguished, grief-stricken howl, like a wolf ululating at the moon. We were dumbfounded. Then he began to shake. I honestly thought he was about to have a seizure. But he was laughing. Giggling, really. We laughed too; there was nothing else to do.

"A Polish dog," he said, nodding with satisfaction.

By the time the new walls were up and the wiring and plumbing were in place, August hit. As if a nationwide school bell had rung, everyone suddenly decamped, heading for the seaside or country. Giuseppe was frustrated of course. There had already been delays—Sor Vincenzo's city hall contact for quick permits had been off sick—and the work was behind schedule. But asking Italians to postpone their August vacation is like asking them to postpone Christmas; there was nothing to do but take a break with the rest of the nation. Giuseppe decided to join Dario and some friends on a weeklong sailing trip; Flavia was off to Toronto for the summer, where she'd earn more money photocopying at my brother's law firm than I did teaching high school.

The day before everyone left, Miro appeared at our door. Ostensibly he had come by to pick up some brushes, but he hung around until it finally dawned on us that he wanted to talk. It was about money. He needed to pay Choo-choo's wages, he explained, be reimbursed for some paint and get an advance for upcoming expenses.

"Oh, I thought some of the advance we gave Sor Vincenzo went to you," I said, embarrassed that no one had thought of this sooner. We'd paid Sor Vincenzo a third of the job up front, out of which he was to pay Miro.

Giuseppe cleared his throat. "Some did."

"I need the second instalment," said Miro.

"But you haven't done two-thirds of the job," I pointed out. He'd barely started, really. "I think we should wait until you've done some more, no?"

Miro fixed me with an indecipherable look—pleading, despair, hostility, maybe all three. He had the usual problems people in his situation had: dependent relatives back home, health issues, loans to be repaid or late being paid back.

I turned to Giuseppe. "Shouldn't we talk this over with Sor Vincenzo?"

But I knew by the expression on Giuseppe's face that we wouldn't. Open discussion about money in Italy was as welcome as a description of your hemorrhoids. Giuseppe would rather take care of the matter discreetly. That afternoon he met Miro at a bar near his bank and gave him the money.

It was a luxurious relief to be alone in Rome in August, with its heat and silence and emptiness. I hadn't realized how cramped I'd been feeling by the constant presence of the workers forging ahead with Giuseppe's archetypal domestic vision.

In the mornings I read in bed or had coffee with the odd friend who'd remained in the city. One day I spent a whole afternoon in the cool of the cellar sorting through our boxes, intending to get rid of some stuff. I wasn't very efficient at it, getting sidetracked by the kids' scrapbooks and artwork and by my journals from when I was new to Italy. They were full of first impressions, loose threads of thought: one-paragraph sketches of people, notes about food and tastes and odors, descriptions of colors or conversations that I'd found quirky or instructive. The haphazard observations of someone passing through a place she didn't expect to end up in. Reading them made me wonder about myself. Not back then, but now. I wondered if I'd really changed much—if I was capable of anything more than a kind of formless wandering through experience, getting lost in the pleasure of observation without much thought of where I was headed—and I wasn't sure.

That night was unbearably hot. I pushed the windows and shutters wide open, hoping to entice a cross-breeze. But none came. I lay awake until dawn, shifting and turning, listening to the soft rustle of the plastic sheeting.

Fabio and Sor Vincenzo returned the first week of September looking like buns just out of the oven, soft and brown and expansive. Sor Vincenzo had gone *in villeggiatura*—to his family's land in the country—and brought us a huge basket of fresh figs, which Giuseppe planned to wrap in prosciutto and serve with Chianti as soon as Miro and Choo-choo got back.

But Miro didn't show up. We were worried of course, and part of my concern, though Giuseppe wouldn't admit he shared it, was that Miro had flown the coop with our money. Fabio finally got hold of Choo-choo, who conveyed in his broken Italian that Miro had had some crisis, maybe health-related. He didn't know where he was or when he'd be coming back to work.

I assumed it was a drinking binge. I knew the others did too; after all, we'd witnessed his vermouth-induced canine transformation. But saying it out loud would have been in bad taste. When I asked each morning if they'd heard from Miro, Fabio just looked tense and Sor Vincenzo shook his head, shrugged and said, "Let's hope he shows up."

"I think Sor Vincenzo should know about the money," I said to Giuseppe after almost two weeks. "Either Miro comes back or we need a replacement. He can't string us along like this."

"Let's just give it a couple more days," he said.

Renovations

After three weeks, Miro reappeared. His skin had a pale, vitreous quality, as if he'd been soaking in bleach, and he'd lost some weight. He smiled his elusive closed-mouth smile, but said nothing. Apart from my over-hearty "Welcome back!" no one gave a hint that we'd been wondering where he was. Miro got to work right away, applying the base coat to the fresh walls and bossing Choo-choo around just as before.

We didn't have much time before the new hardwood floors were scheduled to be laid, and the walls had to be painted first. Giuseppe went to the paint store and came back with a ring of color chips. He showed me the ones he'd selected.

"But they're all white," I said, which was more or less true; some had a barely detectable hint of blue or beige.

"White is classic," he said. "Simple. Elegant."

"Right."

"And light."

"I was thinking maybe we could try some color."

Giuseppe frowned. "Really? How much color?"

I didn't know; I hadn't thought about it. But I didn't want white. Every Italian apartment interior was white.

"Enough to see," I said.

"Like a grey, maybe?"

I took the ring and thumbed through the chips. It was the first time I'd asked him to alter his plans and I knew he was making an effort to be open-minded.

"All right," he said, clearing his throat. "A little color. Why not."

Miro greeted the prospect of color with jittery enthusiasm, as if it were a slightly risqué, avant-garde endeavor. I brought up a stack of art and photography books and together we flipped through them, looking for ideas. As a concession to Giuseppe I picked out light shades—minty green, pale peach, lilac blue—and found matching paint chips. I handed them to Miro one morning and watched him motor off to the paint store on his battered old Vespa. When I came home that afternoon, pallid squares of painted plywood checkered our living-room floor.

I mulled them over for days, switching them around, holding them up to different light, draping scarves over them to see them with accents. But I couldn't decide. The others could—Giuseppe, of course, chose the lightest shades, and Dario liked one that had looked mint on the chip but turned out a weird lizard yellow-green. Flavia, who had returned from Toronto and was back at her friend's for another month, dropped by to choose a color—light blue—for her room. She picked the colors she liked best for the other rooms in about three seconds.

"Just choose," she told me.

Even Choo-choo had his favorites.

Miro was the only one as undecided as I was. He paced up and down, trembling more than usual, I thought. Finally he scowled and said, "These are colors to paint a baby's room. They say nothing." He pointed to one of the photography books, one on India. "Why not choose something from there?"

I picked it up and thumbed through the pages of saffrons and ochres and indigos. They were about as far from white as you could get.

"Let me think about it," I said.

I came home the next day to find the entire living room painted a flushed terra cotta. Miro stood, twitching and nodding. "Once I started, I couldn't stop," he said. "I thought, now *this* Signora Melissa will like. Like that skirt you always wear."

It was beautiful—rich and warm and sensuous. It was a room I could spend the rest of my life in.

When Giuseppe stepped into the living room that evening he froze and blinked. Then he backed out of the room, came back in and stood for a few minutes. He left and re-entered.

Finally he nodded. "I think it works."

"Are you sure?"

"Yes, I'm sure," he smiled. "I like it. A lot."

"I love it."

I pulled Giuseppe into a hug.

"You're not going to believe this," I said, "but Miro chose it."

"Miro?"

"Yeah. Miro. Full of surprises."

Deciding on the other colors was effortless. I handed the chips of yellow ochre and burnt umber and indigo to Miro, and he and Choo-choo turned into painting *virtuosi*, showing up at the crack of dawn and rolling the paint on straight through into the evening. In the arch of a week, our apartment went from looking like a modern art gallery between shows to an Indian bazaar.

On Sunday Flavia came over for our inaugural lunch in the new kitchen.

"Holy shit," she said. "What the hell did you do?"

"I chose."

"Did you ever."

I was still undecided about the front entrance, but I was toying with a deep red from the India book.

"Bordello red," said Dario, smirking. "What does dad think?"

"It's called madder," I said. "The color of the robes of Persian royalty."

Giuseppe glanced at it but didn't say anything. When the kids had left he asked, "Did you pick that red or did Miro?"

"I did," I said, a little hurt. "I picked all the colors except the first one."

"Just thought I'd ask."

Miro and Choo-choo spent the last week applying semigloss to the trim. All that remained to do was the final clean-up and removing the tape from the windowpanes. Miro recommended we hire some "very good cleaners" he knew. A few days later he showed up with a battalion of thick-armed Polish ladies. Rita, a large, dark-haired woman with crystal-blue eyes, shook my hand and told me what they charged per hour, no Italian beating about the bush. Then they got to work, going at the windows like they were purging souls of sin. One woman was particularly merciless and kept cracking the small panes on the older windows as she scrubbed them. Miro stepped in like a factory boss and scolded her in Polish. The next day she'd been demoted to sweeping and Choo-choo was working on replacing the broken panes.

Each evening after everyone had cleared out, Giuseppe inspected what had been done, bending down to make note of a blob of white that had landed on a colored wall or a splatter the women had missed on the windows. Despite his fastidiousness, I could tell he was pleased.

That Saturday night, we celebrated with the workers. Giuseppe spent the day overseeing pasta sauces and vegetable and meat dishes and in the late afternoon went down to the cellar to pull out a couple of choice bottles of champagne.

The men showed up in jackets and ties, Sor Vincenzo with a dessert his wife had made and a beaming Fabio holding a gigantic plant as a housewarming gift. We popped open a bottle while we waited for Miro and Choo-choo. When the buzzer finally rang, it was Choo-choo by himself, with gelled hair and cologne that smelled like a fruit market. Miro had stood him up.

We had a good time anyway, stuffing our faces and arguing over politics. Still, Miro's absence was a faint, disappointing chord. But the next afternoon he appeared, buzzing just as we were finishing the leftovers.

He stood in our doorway with an odd, hangdog look, offering no explanation about his absence the night before. He'd come to talk about money, he said. He'd underestimated how long painting our apartment would take and he wanted a top-up.

"How much of a top-up?" I asked.

"Five hundred euros."

A big top-up. I turned to Giuseppe, ready to stall his usual acquiescence. "I think we should try to reach a compromise."

But Giuseppe shook his head, not at me but at Miro. "No top-up."

He stuck his hand out and shook Miro's. Then he stepped back and shut the door, hard.

It was the first time I'd ever seen Giuseppe be rude. I felt worse for him than I did for Miro.

Over the next few months we saw Fabio and Sor Vincenzo a few times—they came back to fix a leaking radiator and to change a couple of old doorknobs that didn't work properly. I asked about Miro and they told me that he was working on someone's country house outside Rome, but that they hadn't seen much of him. Then one evening while I was in the shower, the phone rang. When I came out Giuseppe was sitting on the living-room couch.

"That was Sor Vincenzo," he said, looking up with bright, stunned eyes. "Some bad news."

"What?"

"Miro died."

"*Died?*" I dropped down beside him. "How?"

"He had a heart attack. His girlfriend found him lying on the floor. Last night. She hadn't seen him for a couple of days."

"Miro had a girlfriend?"

"One of the cleaners." Of course, Rita, the blue-eyed beauty.

We sat together, staring at our walls—the yellow ochre through the kitchen doorway, the burnt umber of the corridor, the terra cotta of the living room. All I could think of was Miro's house in the Polish woods of his childhood.

"But his house wasn't finished yet," I said.

Giuseppe nodded and took my hand, holding it tightly but not saying anything.

We drove to the Rome morgue the next day and with Sor Vincenzo and Fabio watched as the workers welded shut Miro's metal casket and placed it in the outer, wooden coffin. Choo-choo and Rita showed up a little later. Rita pulled me into her arms and clasped me as we cried. I asked if she'd contacted Miro's sons, but she said they'd been estranged for years, that a sister in Cracow was arranging the burial. A priest came by and recited a blessing and it was over.

On the way home Giuseppe said, "I paid for his body to be shipped back to Poland. His top-up." He gave a sad smile.

Earlier in the summer, when I was cleaning out the cellar, I'd come across an essay that Giuseppe had written in high school. It was an assignment from religion class, some teacher's effort to get the kids interested in the Bible: "If you'd been present at the Last Supper, what role would you have liked to play?" I pictured Giuseppe, no great believer, politely correcting Christ's grammar or suggesting a better way to express "blood of the covenant." But he had taken the question seriously and written that he would have cleaned up after the meal—cleared the table, swept and put things away. How what gave him the most satisfaction was seeing something finished properly.

It occurred to me that some people attained this sense of completion in what they did, were able to give their lives meaning through form. And that since I first noticed him at the *cineforum*, it wasn't his part in the action that had attracted me, as I'd then believed, but the care he took in shaping it.

I also realized that other people drifted along, finding meaning in small bursts. Often a little surprised at where life took them, a little slow to understand why.

Acknowledgements

For their unwavering support, generosity and careful reading, I'm particularly grateful to Kitty Wolfe, Brigid Grauman, Jyl McDougal, Laura Tate and Virginia Mak.

For their help in different, important ways, thank you also to Paola Cosentino, Deborah Cowman, Donna Ducharme, Cindi Emond, Elisabeth Etue, Olivia Ercoli, Bruce Fernie, Antonio Ficarra, Chris Lowry, the late Judith Merrill, Claudia Neri, Frank Paci, Gilbert Reid, Sheila Stewart and my wonderful Roman compatriots at CWAR.

Thanks as well to Charis Wahl and Carolyn Wood for their thoughtful editorial assistance.

Andrea, Michael, Mark, Betty and John Williams have been encouraging from the very start; my heartfelt gratitude.

Grazie di cuore a Gemma e all'insostituibile Carlo Vallecchi, amante dei racconti; alla famiglia Zavota di Parma; e a Maddalena e Ginevra, per tutta la loro fiducia ed il loro amore.

An especial thank-you to Margie Wolfe, *donna straordinaria*, for her infectious cackle and gentle pushing.

My deepest gratitude to Lorenzo Vallecchi, love of my life, *per tutto.*